Wicked Little Rabbit

Samantha Moran

Obsidian Inkwell Publishing

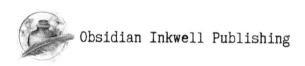 Obsidian Inkwell Publishing

Published by Obsidian Inkwell Publishing, LLC
www.obsidianinkwell.com

Titles: *Wicked Little Rabbit* / Samantha Moran
Description: Hardcover First Edition
Publication Date: April 30, 2024
Cover Design: Samantha Moran (Canva)
Formatting: Samantha Moran (Vellum)

Hardcover ISBN-13: 978-1-959751-17-5
Also available in ebook, paperback, and special editions.

TABLE OF CONTENTS

BONUS CONTENT

DEDICATION

For Kassie.
Sometimes, the horrors that go bump in the night are enticing.
Sometimes, they should be left alone.

NOTE FROM THE AUTHOR

Wicked Little Rabbit is a supernatural horror and psychological thriller reimagining of Lewis Carroll's *Alice in Wonderland,* a book in the public domain. As such, this book will contain explicit and disturbing scenes. Due to this, *Wicked Little Rabbit* is intended for mature audiences only (18+). Please proceed with caution.

This book contains passages with strong language and content related to: dubious consent, rape (especially chapters twenty-three and twenty-five), evisceration, pseudo-cannibalism, kidnapping, medical trauma, mental illness, self-harm, alcoholic substances, drug use, inaccurate BDSM, blood, death, and more. If any of these topics are disturbing to you, you may not wish to proceed with this text.

Due to the nature of this content, resources for sexual assault survivors have been included at the end of this text.

The broken grammar used to convey the main character's fragile mental state is stylistic and intentional.

Should you decide to continue with this text, thank you for reading *Wicked Little Rabbit,* the first installment in the For the Dark and Depraved series. I hope you enjoy this twisted tale.

WICKED LITTLE TUNES

Want to listen to a playlist inspired by Wicked Little Rabbit? Scan this QR code and find it on YouTube! Happy hauntings and happy listening!

Wicked Little Rabbit

"Somehow you strayed and lost your way, and now there'll be no time to play, no time for joy, no time for friends — not even time to make amends."

— LEWIS CARROLL, AN EXCERPT FROM *ALICE'S ADVENTURES IN WONDERLAND*, 1865

CHAPTER 1
NOW

HUSHED WHISPERS. MORE THAN ONE. MAYBE TWO? THREE? CAN'T TELL. They're outside. Outside of the room.

Not my room. Not my house. Not home at all.

Had home? Maybe. *Think so?* Not sure. Can't recall.

Understand idea. A safe space. A haven. Comfortable. Mine.

Not this. Not at home. Just here. The room where they keep me. Lock me up. Hide me away.

Prison cell.

No, not real prison. Not jail. No bars. Something different. Something clinical. Sterile.

But, where?

I… I don't know.

Nowhere is safe. Not now. Not like this. Home is forgotten. A dream.

Why? Why no memory? *What's happened?* How?

Rummage through bits and pieces. Everything broken. Loose threads. Mind torn. Unraveling. Falling apart.

So much pain. Can't concentrate. Thoughts too broken.

Head hurts. Feels wrong. Too much inside. Too much… missing? Doesn't make sense.

Can't… Can't think. Figure it out. Distracted by noise.

Buzzing.

All around me. Vibration consuming room. Like hornets in ears. Wasps in brain. Crawling on skin. Piercing like needles. Igniting nerves. Invisible. Swarming.

Hiding in lights. Much too bright. Stab at my pupils. Irritate. Never off.

Need to shut them out. To close eyes. Make them go away. If only for moment.

Can't control them. Lids resist. Glued open. Held by silent command. Instinctual.

Have to see. To watch. To keep guard. To protect.

Protect from what?

Anxiety rises. One thought clear enough.

In case it happens. Again. In case she comes. Finds me. Keeps promise.

She, who?

New sensation now. Scalp burns like fire. Fingers in my hair. Pulling tight. Too tight. Threatening to rip roots free from skull.

Momentary panic. Stomach flips. Bones turn to jelly. Muscles tremble.

Retreat. Scoot away from bed. As fast as I can. Slam into flat surface. Wall.

Cower and groan.

Realize they're mine. My fingers. My hands. My unrelenting grip.

Blow out breath. Shove hysteria down.

Keep calm. Impossible to do. Steady self. *Don't break down.*

My fingers, remind body. *My hands. Not hers. Still alone.*

Back taps wall. Rhythmic thumps. Rock. Rock. Rock. Rock. Rock.

Voices again. Closer. Clearer. Louder.

Stop moving. Freeze. Statue of stone.

Sit still. Quiet breathing. Listen. Wait.

Ping! Metallic sound. Lock clicks. Mechanism releases.

Door cracks. Just a sliver. A gateway. *To where?* What lies beyond?

Heart pounds. Heavy beats on rapid drums. Breath sticks in chest. Lungs seize. Blood surges through body. Skin grows cold. Icy. Adrenaline courses in veins.

Slowly opens. Swinging in. Inch by inch by inch.

No… No, no, no…

Don't look away. See what's coming. Must know.

Nausea swirls. Rising in throat. Swallow it down. Can't let it escape Not now.

Door always closed. Sealed tight since they carried me in. No handle inside. No windows. Can't see out.

Just this box. All white… everywhere. Walls. Ceiling. Bed. Floor.

Keeps me in. Yes. Not good. Can't run. Nowhere to go.

But, keeps *them* out. Keeps her away. Can't find me. Can't see me. Can't touch me. Take me to the dark places. Drain any more.

Not *safe* in here… but *safer* when closed.

Safety gone.

Door opens. All the way. Big gap. Too much hole.

Man steps inside. Small. Looks grim. Khaki pants. Button-down shirt. Leather shoes. Curly hair. Brown. Clean shaven. Pale complexion. Freckles. Big blue eyes. Magnified by lenses. Pushes glasses up nose and studies me.

Then, another. This one bigger. Black hair. Not as pale. Much wider. All muscles. Broad shoulders. Legs like trunks. Stubble on cheeks and chin.

Oh, fuck. Fuck! Need to get out. Out of this room. Right now. Out of their reach.

Big one blocks door. Can't do it. No escape. Couldn't get past. No other exit. Trapped in here. With them. Strangers. Dangerous.

Screwed.

Whimper. Let go of hair. Try to scoot away. Search for place to hide.

No dark corners. No barriers. No grooves. Only bed. But, too far away. Too close to small one. Wouldn't get there in time.

Big one closes door. Lock thunks. Seals us in. Stays there. Crosses arms over chest. Feet wide.

Little one moves closer. Slow steps. Cautious. Slight frown.

Bring knees to chest. Tuck head down behind them. Wrap arms around self. Guard all I can.

Peer through gap in legs. Watch little one closely.

Crouches down. Few feet away. Puts weight on toes. Shoes crease. Holds hands up. Signal of peace. Eyebrows raise. Shoulders drop.

"Hello. I'm Dr. Barrows." Quiet voice. Gentle. He waits.

Don't respond. Hope he'll leave. Pull knees in tighter. Heels touch my bottom.

Doesn't go. Sits down on floor. Crisscrosses legs. Casual. Motionless.

Still too close. Uncomfortable.

Big one shifts. Adjusts stance. Movement draws my eyes.

Won't look at me. Not sure why. Wears stoic frown. Drops one arm to side. Nightstick there. Weapon. In reach. Puts other hand on hip. Watches doctor. Keeps door behind him.

"I'm told you've been through significant trauma," Doctor tries. "I'm so sorry for that. No one should have to experience such things."

Trauma? Feels right. True. Explains fear. Pain.

Doctor continues. "Please, know that I will not hurt you. I am not your enemy. Whatever you have been through happened beyond these walls. I am aware that this does not change things, but in this room, you are safe."

Liar. Not safe. Never safe again.

Don't say anything. Keep mouth closed. Don't dare speak.

"I want to help you," Doctor adds. "That's my job."

Waits for response. Give him none.

"The man behind me is Andrew. He's my assistant, here for my protection. We work as a team, he and I. For now, I have instructed him to wait by the door unless he is needed. He won't speak to you or intervene unless my well-being is endangered. Do you understand?"

Big one has name. Andrew. *Andrew the guard.*

Finally looks at me. Gray eyes. Dark. Blank. Hard.

Gray eyes good. Blue, too. Not like hers. Not yellow. Not gold. Like molten metal. Not red. Color of blood.

Big one seems to make decision. Nods in my direction. Takes hand off hip. Moves other arm away from nightstick. Shuffles again. Leans against door. Relaxes some.

"We are about to begin a journey together, you and I." Doctor clasps hands. Intertwines fingers. "Hopefully, the two of us will be able to uncover the truth of what has occurred, of who you are and how this happened. But to help you, I need to know that you comprehend the things I am saying when we talk. That's crucial. Healing is not a one-way street, especially not in circumstances like yours."

Lift head from knees. Narrow eyes. Furrow brow.

"My colleagues tell me that you can speak. I'll understand if you're not comfortable doing so with me yet. Trust takes time to develop. We will build that relationship at your pace. But, in the meantime, we will need some way to communicate with each other. So, how about we try this? If you understand what I am saying to you, why don't we start with a nod. Just a simple nod. Can you do that for me?"

A nod. Wants me to nod…

Room is silent. No one speaks. Andrew watches doctor. Doctor watches me. Patiently waits. Inspects.

Slowly, start to breathe. Let lungs expand.

"Can you nod for me if you understand?" Doctor repeats question.

Body answers for me. Nods head on own.

Didn't expect to. Hadn't meant to. Action surprises me. Catches me off guard.

Shrink away from Doctor. Make self small. Small as I can.

Joints twinge. Reawakens senses. Hurts to sit here. To hold self so tightly.

Hard to focus. Too much strain. Lights blind. Head throbs.

"Good. That's an excellent start." Doctor unbuttons cuffs at wrists. Reveals shiny watch. Reflection flashes. Second hand ticks. Ticks. Ticks. "It's important for us to be able to communicate if this is going to work. So, let's continue with nods for now if that is best for you. If I ask you a question and the answer is yes, you can nod again. Or, if I say something you agree with, you can nod then, too. But, if I say something you disagree with or ask a question and the answer is no, you can shake your head to indicate otherwise. Okay?"

Consider his words. Wants to talk to me. *Do I? Want to talk? Communicate?*

Maybe. Says he will help. Need help. So much help.

Hesitate. Waver. Finally decide.

Nod again. Might as well. Already knows I can.

Thinking too much. So tired.

Finally, lids come unglued.

Eyes close. Long blink. Too long. Threaten to stay that way.

Feels good. They're dry. Bruised. Gritty like sandpaper.

Sleep calls.

No. No, no, no, no! Tear them open. Too easy to let go. To drift off.

No more closing. Not for more than a second.

Doctor notices reaction. Hint of concern on features. Doesn't say anything about it. Keeps going. "I appreciate that you're giving me this opportunity. It takes a lot of courage, and I find that admirable. Perhaps, it will help if I tell you a little more about myself?"

Posed as question. Not really question. More like invitation. Straighten up more.

"Allow me to further introduce myself. As I said, I'm Dr. Barrows. I'm a psychiatrist here at St. Ambrose Hospital. That's where you are. You were brought in early this morning." Lets words sink in. "I work with individuals like yourself and try to help them regain control over their situations when their minds seem to have gotten a little lost."

Overhead, one light flickers. Surprises me. Makes me jump.

Doctor looks up. Surprised him, too. Narrows eyes at fixture. Doesn't blink again. Steadies. Doctor turns back to me.

"I am pleased to meet you, though of course, I wish it was under different circumstances. I would love to allow you to introduce your-self, but my colleagues tell me we have not yet been able to learn your name." Pauses. Sad smile. "Do you know your name?"

Name? My name. *Have a name?* Should know that. It's mine…

Doctor has a name. Doctor Barrows. Guard has a name. Andrew.

My name?

Shake head. Missing. Can't find it. Vanished.

Too much thinking. Buzzing comes again. Had been gone since Doctor started talking. So loud now. So distracting. Room spins like carnival ride.

"That's quite alright. Please don't feel pressured. We'll figure it out together. But, I would certainly like to be able to call you something. It feels inhumane to refer to you as 'the patient' or 'John Doe,' as the police so often do to those in your position. I'm certain that won't allow us to foster the connection we'll need going forward." Doctor sighs. Grasps chin. Rubs thumb and finger along jaw. Muses. "Could we choose a temporary name? Something of a placeholder? How would you feel about that?"

Blink at Doctor. Attempt to process his words. Struggle to comprehend.

Wants to give me name? Would feel nice. To have name. To be person. Have something to hold on to. Easier.

Slow nod. Unsure.

"Wonderful. I believe that would be beneficial to both of us. Well, what should we call you for now?"

Doctor looks at me. Don't know. Glances at Andrew. Andrew shrugs.

"How about something rather common. Would it be okay if I called you James?"

James. James. James. James.

Agree with Doctor. Not my name. Feels wrong. Sounds wrong. But, okay for now.

Be James. Can do that.

"James it is. At least, for the time being. As soon as we learn your true identity, we can make the change. That will be much better." Doctor turns to Andrew. "When we leave, will you please inform the staff that this is the name we've decided upon?"

"Yes, Doctor Barrows."

"Thank you, Andrew. Now, for our first order of business." Doctor pauses. Eyes travel from my head to toes. Discerning. Speaks again. "How are you feeling, James? Are you in any pain?"

Pain. So much pain. Getting worse every minute. Pain in eyes. Pain in ears. Pain in nose. In jaw. In throat. Unbearable.

Nod. Nod vigorously. Brain rattles in skull. Bounces off bone. Keep nodding until Doctor holds up hands in worry.

"Alright, I understand. I'm so sorry to hear that, James. The staff noticed a number of bruises when you arrived. If you could, would you show me where in particular you're hurting? I'd like to give you something to take it away, but I need to be sure I know what's happening first."

Fingers fly back to hair. Dig into scalp. Tug once more at strands. Stare at Doctor. Hope he sees. Comprehends.

"Your head hurts, James? Is that correct?" he asks. Gestures at his own.

Nod again. Makes room spin faster. Feel unstable. Brings back nausea. Stronger now. Sour. Copper taste.

Swallow. Remind self to breathe.

"We can give you some medicine for your head. Would you like that? Perhaps, even something to help you sleep?"

Eyes widen in fear. Blood drains from face. Ice takes hold of bones.

No. No sleeping!

Shake head. Deny. Curl further into self.

Need to be in control. Can't black out. Can't give in.

She'll come. Warned me. She'll find me.

Doctor frowns. "No medicine, James? None at all?"

Shake head once more.

"I'm trying to understand. Please, bear with me. Let's work through your concerns." Thinks for a moment, then asks, "Are you afraid to go to sleep?"

Yes! Nod. Several times. Tears bead lashes.

"I see. I'm sorry for my misinterpretation. We have other options. Would you rather something to dull your discomfort? A nonsedative?"

Dull pain? Pain means distraction. Distraction means vulnerable. Less pain means clearer. Better. Easier to focus. To protect self.

Lick cracking lips. Wet them. Only barely. Mouth too dry.

Agree reluctantly.

"Help me." Words escape me. No time to stop them.

Doctor's eyes grow. Surprise. Touch of delight. "I'm glad to hear you speak, James. Thank you for that. And, thank you for allowing me to assist you with your pain. I will do my best to make you more comfortable without sedation." Smiles at me. Proud of progress. "Andrew will need to aid me for a moment if that's alright. He and I will step outside to retrieve the medicine I promised and return momentarily."

Say nothing. No more speaking. No more answers. No more.

Doctor stands. Watches my reaction. Doesn't turn away. Backs toward the door.

Lowers voice and mumbles something to Andrew. Can't make out his words.

Andrew looks at me. Grimaces. Glances back to Doctor.

"Give him all the medicine you want," Andrew whispers. A little too loud. "But, I've got a feeling about this one. It's not gonna help. He's mad as a hatter."

Doctor's expression falls. Disappointed. "Kindness, Andrew," he admonishes. "This man has been through something horrific. We are not here to judge. We are here to listen, as you should well know."

Andrew looks guilty. Emotion passes quickly. "Kindness is great, but security is more important. Watch your back, Doctor Barrows. He's feral. My gut always knows."

Presses flat object to exit. Lock clicks. Door swings open again.

Flash of anger on Doctor's face. Not at me. At Andrew.

"We will return momentarily, James. I promise," Doctor claims. "We aren't leaving you. Not for long. Just stepping away." Seems sincere.

Watch them leave. Door closes behind. Room empty again.

Once more alone.

Crawl across floor to crevice under bed. Slide inside cramped space. Retreat as far as possible.

Mattress blocks light. Soothes eyes. Calms nerves.

Shadows hold me. Wrap me in embrace. Keep me away from the door.

"James," I mumble. Gritted teeth. Tight jaw. "James." I repeat. Try to hold on.

Hiding doesn't fix pain. Throbbing too much. Pressure building. Consuming. Torturing.

Can't handle anymore.

Make it stop. Make it stop. Make it stop.

Beat head against tile.

Help! Help me! Help…

Room fills with screams. Don't recognize at first. Agonized, harsh sounds. Pitiful noises. Whimpers. Awful. Horrible.

Mine. Belong to me. My voice.

"No more!" I roar.

Can't live like this. Not living. Barely surviving.

Death would be kinder.

CHAPTER 2

THEN

"Alright. This is getting ridiculous." Braxton rolls his neck and groans. Frustration washes off of him in waves. "How long have we been at this?"

"How should I know?" I ask. Narrowly dodging an opponent's blast, I maneuver my player into an outcropping, away from enemy fire. "Respawn and get back over here. I'm dying. I need a healer."

Braxton raises an eyebrow, ignoring the game. "Literal hours, dude. And, you haven't moved from that spot. Not even to piss. This has gone on long enough."

"The hell it has. I've almost got this." As soon as I haul my character out of its hiding place, an explosion sends it flying into a jagged stone wall. "Fuck! Come on, man! I'm so close."

"That's what she said," he jests. An impish grin spreads across his face.

He wants me to laugh at his stupid joke. I'm too invested in the screen to care. "The target is right there. Seriously, don't be a douche. Let's go!"

"Nah, you're done. Playtime is over." Braxton mashes the pause button, and the game freezes, bringing up the start menu. Snatching my controller out of my hand, he adds, "We're going out."

Thoroughly pissed off, I collapse against the cushions. "I already told you no."

"And, I told you I don't care. Get the fuck off the couch and get dressed, asshole. It's time to be an adult now. You know, leave the house."

Braxton tosses our controllers onto the coffee table. They land with solid thuds. One of them skids to the edge, then falls to the floor. A pile of empty candy wrappers follows in its wake. The joystick crushes into the carpet. On the screen, his avatar jerks, jumping around pointlessly. The game's theme music plays on a loop in the background.

"Seriously?" I gesture at the mess. "Those are expensive. I just bought that one. It's a limited edition."

"I don't give two shits. Jesus, man. It's so damn depressing seeing you sit here and mope," he complains.

"I'm not fucking moping." Yes, I am. But, that's beside the point. I don't want to give him the satisfaction. "I've been busy."

He knows it's a lie, and it's not even a good one. I've made up better stories to call into work.

Whatever. I'm not taking his shit tonight.

"Yeah? With what, Cinderella?" His gaze travels over my stained sweatpants and ratty t-shirt. "Too busy scrubbing floors?"

Maybe he has a point. When was the last time I washed these? A week ago? They're starting to smell.

God, that's just downright disgusting.

Braxton stands and stretches his arms over his head, then turns to face me. In the television's dim light, his dark hair is as black as oil. Shadows cut across his features, settling into the hollows of his eyes and below his cheekbones, giving him an almost skeletal appearance.

"Name one good reason you can't go out with me tonight instead of wasting your time holed up in this apartment with all the lights off."

"If I beat this boss, I unlock a new gun. That's as good a reason as any."

Braxton scoffs. "What are you? A nerd?" He picks up an empty beer can and shakes it, then gives it a sniff. The spoiled scent makes him cringe. "This is just sad, man. What happened to you? I mean, I know she called it off, but did Celeste take your dick with her when she left?"

He tosses the empty can in my direction like an accusation. I swat it away, not caring where it lands. It skitters across the living room floor and splashes rancid liquid onto the sliding glass door.

"My dick is fine. Wanna take it for a test drive? Climb on up."

Braxton eyes me with irritation. Not wanting to continue this line of questioning, I snatch a cold piece of pizza from the grease-soaked box on the coffee table and stuff it into my mouth.

"It's been three weeks. All you do is go to work and come home and play video games. I like games as much as the next guy, but you need to get laid or else you'll be the weird dude who forgets how to talk to women and winds up in his mother's basement. Do you want that?"

"My mother doesn't have a basement," I say around my mouthful of cheese and sausage. "And, this is my apartment. Your argument is invalid."

"Quit fucking dodging the point," he commands, exasperated. He stalks over to the light switch and snaps it on, making me squint.

"No." It's a simple response, but it makes my position clear enough.

Braxton rolls his eyes and shakes his head. He checks his watch, then flicks his gaze from his wrist to me. Expression hardening, he turns and heads for the bathroom, addressing me over his shoulder. "I don't care if you want to go out or not. That's too damn bad. You've got ten minutes, man. Long enough for me to take a decent shit. If you're not dressed and ready to go by then, I'm calling for a welfare check. They'll haul you out of this dump kicking and screaming, and I'll make sure they drag your ass off to the psych ward. Try me."

I open my mouth to respond, but he doesn't wait for me to answer. He just walks away, disappearing around the corner. A moment later, the sound of the bathroom door closing booms through my place.

Shutting my eyes, I let my head fall back against the couch and groan, contemplating my options.

I don't want to go to the goddamn bar. That's Braxton's solution for everything. Get wasted, get laid, and get the fuck over it. He dragged me to the strip club when my college girlfriend broke up with me during her study abroad semester. Somehow, I wound up in a night-club three states over when my dog died. Who knows what he has planned now that my fiancée is gone, too? We might end up in Vegas, three sheets to the wind, married to some chicks we met at the airport and broke as the day is long.

But, annoying as he may be, Braxton is a man of his word. If I don't do what I'm told, he really will call the cops. He'd do it just to prove that he could. I wouldn't even have time to hide my stash or my bong by the time the cops showed up at my door.

Who am I kidding? I don't have any options. It's my way or his, and his way is so much easier. Why fight him? What's the worst that could happen if I go along with his plan? I get drunk?

I wouldn't be alone this time. Drinking at a bar is acceptable. Crying over my beer can on the couch is pitiful.

He's an ass, but he means well. At least, when it comes to me. I know that. I'm like his little pet, trailing along on his leash. Have been since college. Wherever he goes, I follow. And, he looks out for me. Keeps me from falling apart over stuff like this.

So, no. Braxton is not the kind of man who will let me grieve my loss like a miserable wretch. If I wanted to stay here and wallow in my emotions, I should never have called him in the first place.

Why did I invite him over? I should have left well enough alone.

Because I can't beat this damn level, and it's been five days.

Fuck me, how pathetic is that?

Ugh, he's right. My life *has* become a joke since Celeste left. I'm twenty-nine, and I've practically reverted into a moody teenager.

Whatever. Let's get this over with, then. The night is young, but the clock is ticking. He probably set a damn timer on his phone.

Begrudgingly, I wipe my sweaty hands on my pants and climb out of my seat. Grumbling under my breath every step of the way, I stalk to my bedroom, annoyed but resolved.

He must hear me coming because he shouts, "Put on some damn deodorant. Cologne, too. You stink of desperation, dude. No one wants to smell that shit."

"You're an asshole!" I yell before I shut the door.

Braxton's laugh cuts through the barrier like it's made of butter. "Say whatever you want, but you'll thank me in the morning."

CHAPTER 3
THEN

I DON'T KNOW HOW BRAXTON FOUND THIS PLACE. IT'S A LITERAL HOLE IN the wall tucked inside the mouth of an alley. The only indication there's even a club here is a nondescript steel door set into the worn brick of an old warehouse wall. There's no sign or logo anywhere to be found. Overhead, a faded billboard claims this used to be a meat processing plant. The huge banner advertising "Ronaldo's Steaks and Prime Cuts" has been ravaged by time. It hangs in shreds that flap in the wind, ready to tear off and blow away at any moment.

I'll give it this much: the venue has good soundproofing. The street it's on is nearly dead silent. Most bars can be heard from several blocks away. Not this one. I swear, if you tried hard enough, you could hear a pin drop from down the road.

No cars pass by as we draw closer. There's no traffic at all, actually. The only noise is a faint buzzing emanating from what are supposed to be streetlights. The droning sets my teeth on edge. It's only electricity, but it reminds me of wasps, and I fucking hate those little bastards. For whatever reason, they love me, though.

Regardless, for the last five blocks we've walked, none of the lamps have worked. I had to use my phone's flashlight to avoid tripping over raised sections of sidewalk.

Braxton found this hilarious. I found it annoying.

I'd expected to see a line of partiers outside the building, but there's no one waiting to get in. A single bouncer stands out front, arms crossed over his chest, surveying the street. He's big and bulky, but he's wearing sunglasses at night. Plus, his striped t-shirt is way too fucking tight. It squeezes his biceps so hard, I bet it's cutting off his circulation.

Douche move. Compensation 101.

No one respects a hipster barring the gate or a man in child's clothing. Sure, he's jacked, but I can't help but wonder if he can see anything at all through those dark lenses. Does his semi-straitjacket slow his reflexes? Not much of a guard if he can't handle the rabble, is he?

"Antonio!" Braxton offers in greeting as we approach. His face lights up with mischief. There's a glimmer in his eyes that warns of trouble. "How's it hanging, man?"

"Same way it was last time, dipshit. ID?" Antonio, who I suspect is not *really* named Antonio at all, wants nothing to do with Braxton's games.

Braxton scoffs. "You know who I am, yet you do this every time. Do I really need to dig out my wallet?"

"We follow the laws at this establishment. ID, or get crawling back to your gutter. I'm not asking a third time."

"Yeah, I'm aware."

Braxton elbows me in the ribs. *God, he's bony.* There'll be a bruise there in the morning.

"Do the man a solid, will you? Whip it out. I don't want to stand out here all night."

Obliging my friend, I dig into my back pocket and pull out my metal wallet. He does the same with his leather one. The bouncer snatches our IDs and holds them up close to his face, glancing between us. Satisfied we aren't trying to pull the wool over his eyes, he passes them back. Immediately, his expression shifts to boredom.

"What's it been, a year?" Braxton continues. "I've missed your busted mug."

"A week. Not long enough, I'll tell you that much. Now, shut your fucking mouth before I bust yours up for you."

"Yeah, alright. You don't have to flirt so much." Braxton bats his eyelashes at the security guard. Puckering his lips, he blows the man a suggestive kiss.

Antonio's jaw sets in a hard line in warning. My friend holds up his hands in resignation, then stuffs his wallet back into his pocket. I follow suit.

The bouncer pushes Braxton aside and tugs the solid steel door open. Impossibly loud and heavy bass explodes out into the alleyway. Multi-colored spotlights shine from the ceiling inside the club, but the vast majority of the place is out of sight, blocked behind a three-quarter-height wall that turns to the left.

"Don't get lost," he offers snidely. "I'm not saving your stupid asses."

As we step in, Braxton claps the bouncer on his shoulder like an old buddy. The muscle-bound guard flips him off and slams the door behind us.

"Friend of yours?" I ask. We round the bend and emerge beside a dance floor.

"World's best," he answers, yelling over the music. "Even bought him the mug to prove it. I might ask him to be the best man at my wedding someday."

My face falls. Braxton has the decency to cringe, realizing it's too soon for that kind of joke.

"It's fine. I wasn't going to ask you anyway." I was. "You would have screwed all the bridesmaids, and it would've been my problem when Celeste found out." That much isn't a lie.

"You know me too well." He laughs and ushers me over to the bar. "Hell yeah you would have, though. I'm your wingman. And, that would have been a *glorious* night. Fuck her for taking my shot away, huh?"

There are two empty seats in the middle, so I pull out a stool and sink onto it. Braxton opts to stand and smacks his hands on the sticky oak top.

"My treat, alright?" He drums along to the beat.

"You dragged me out here. I wasn't going to pay for my own drinks. My tab was on you from the moment you threatened me."

He sucks air through his teeth. "*Threat* is a harsh word. More like encouraged. With leverage."

"Extortion."

Braxton chuckles again, but the sound is drowned out by a new song. The overhead lights shift, illuminating more of the dance floor and plunging the bar into shadow.

"Whatever, man. Just do the damn thing. Order yourself something poisonous, knock it back, and get fucked up. This place is packed. You'll have your pick of the ladies. Someone has to be desperate enough to go home with you."

He's right about that. Well, about the crowd, at least. The lack of line outside doesn't match up with the number of people gathered in the once-warehouse. The dance floor is packed. Sweat-soaked bodies grind up against each other, moving to the beat. The few booths lining the walls are all taken. Except for my stool and the one Braxton refuses to acknowledge, it's standing room only.

"Start with her," Braxton commands, raising his finger and pointing at the back of a dirty blonde woman in low-rise jeans and a bright blue club shirt.

"You have got to be kidding me." My eyes widen when I see who he's targeted.

"What?" he asks innocently.

The woman's hair is pulled back into a neat high ponytail, and it swishes as she stoops down to dig a bottle of beer out of the cooler. A small white bow is pinned at the top, which practically glows under the blacklight LEDs that light up the liquor shelves. She's busy talking to a couple at the opposite end of the bar. Lesbians by the look of them. One woman has her arm wrapped possessively around the other, thumb dipped into the latter's shirt pocket. The former accepts the glass bottle, and the second mouths their order. It's drowned out by the insistent rhythm, but the blonde turns back to the tap and pours a dark liquid into a stout glass, letting a thick layer of foam pool on the surface.

"Damn, she gives good head, huh?" Braxton slaps me on the back. He looks entirely too pleased.

"The bartender? Jesus, man. Why?"

"Because she's fucking hot," he answers. He gestures at his face, then back to her. "What, you don't think so?"

"Of course, I do. But, she's the bartender. She's not here for a hookup."

"You don't know that."

"Does she look even remotely interested in going home with anyone to you? Especially me?"

Braxton studies the woman for a moment, then looks at me with a shit-eating grin. "Not yet," he says. "Make her interested."

"That would be hard anyway, but I haven't hit on a girl in years. It ain't gonna happen."

"Not with an attitude like that, it isn't." Before I can stop him, he smacks the bar again and waves his hand in the air. "Hey, beautiful!"

The blonde bartender turns to face Braxton and rolls her eyes.

We're off to a great start here.

"Come on, baby," he calls out. "My friend has a tall order for you."

CHAPTER 4
NOW

"JAMES, CAN YOU HEAR ME?" DOCTOR ASKS. FLASHES PENLIGHT IN FACE. Makes me squint. "The medication I've administered is quite powerful, but I didn't want to take any chances that your pain might not be managed. You've been through enough."

Brain working slowly. Lagging. Grinds, trying to catch up.

Sensations flood through body. Pain dimmed. Something soft beneath me.

Not where I was. Floor isn't soft. Should be hard. Cold.

Face scrunches. Confused.

Doctor notices. "Andrew assisted me in getting you onto your cot. It was difficult to retrieve you from under the bed on my own. I felt it would have been imprudent to tug on your limbs to assist your passage, especially given your condition, and as you know the cot is bolted to the floor for your safety."

In bed? No. Not possible. Not unless…

Did Doctor do it? Knock me out?

So groggy. Crack eyes open. Retreat until back presses against wall. Try to put space between us.

Doctor holds up hands. "You fell asleep of your own accord after the dose took effect. It was not a sedative. You need not worry about that."

Doctor answers question I didn't ask. "I am a man of my word, James. As I said earlier, we're working to build a relationship of trust. I would not deceive you. That would only cause harm. Your body was just tired."

Tired? *Yes.* More than that. Exhausted. Hollow. Drained. *Empty.*

Slept on own? Don't want to sleep. Too risky. Leaves me unguarded.

Doctor sits in chair by bed. Chair that wasn't there before. Must have brought it with him. Leans forward onto arms. Elbows press into white rectangle on lap. Flexible cotton fabric. A pillow.

"I hope you aren't upset about the decision to move you, James. I considered leaving you there, but in the end, I thought it best to transfer you to a more comfortable location. I can't imagine you would have gotten much rest in such a place. Of course, I'm so sorry to have disturbed you if you were."

Sadness on his face. Genuine concern. Mouth turns down at corners. Brow pinched, too. Worried.

"I've brought you a pillow, as well. It's a small luxury, but one I hope you might enjoy, especially since you're experiencing head pain. If you wouldn't mind lifting up for me, I can place it beneath you. Can you do that, James?"

Want to answer. Try to do it. To lift head. To follow Doctor's orders.

Find it difficult. Muscles respond, but only barely. Still worn. Skull too heavy. Lifts maybe an inch. Neck strains, then drops.

Head bounces off mattress. Disorients.

"Would you like me to help you?" Doctor nods. Encourages.

Nod back. Or, something close to it. Not sure he saw it. Body so weak. Wants to shut down.

"Alright. I'm going to reach under your neck, James. But before I do, please remember that I won't hurt you. I'm simply going to raise you up long enough to place the pillow there and put you back down."

Rustling sounds by door. Drag eyes to source.

Andrew waits. Shifts on feet. Closer than he was. Cautious. Keeps watch over Doctor. Not reaching for nightstick. But, tense. Ready.

Doctor's touch is warm. Slips hand under back of head. Careful not to hurt. Lifts me slowly. Slides pillow below. Gently puts me down.

"Good. Thank you for that, James. I want you to know that your comfort is very important. I'm glad you let me help you. I'd like to continue doing so. Please, forgive the lack of pillowcase and blankets. We can't risk providing those yet. After we get to know each other more, I can try to make some arrangements, okay?"

"Okay." Don't bother attempting to move. Voice hoarse. Throat dry. Parched. A desert.

Swallow. Wince.

"Would you like something to drink, James? I can get you some water. Or, Andrew can see about collecting some food for you if you're hungry. Are you hungry, James?

Drag hand up to face. Touch lips. Fingers snag on rough skin. Flaky. "Drink." Let arm fall onto chest.

"Excellent. I can certainly do that for you. Andrew?" Doctor turns to guard. "Would you please grab an unopened water bottle from the nurses? Room temperature, if you don't mind. I'd rather not shock James's system. And, some crackers if you could. That would be great."

"Are you sure you want to be alone with him, Doctor Barrows?" Andrew seems nervous. Eyes narrow. "I'm not sure that's the best choice." Stares at me. Touches fingertips to nightstick.

Doctor frowns. Andrew pulls hand away from baton.

"I'll be quite alright, I assure you." Doctor looks at me. Smiles. "You won't hurt me, right James?"

Nod. No reason to hurt Doctor. He's kind.

"Then, it's settled. The water and crackers please, Andrew. Quick as you can."

Andrew still unsure. Hesitates. Eyes flick between us. Weighs options.

Finally gives in to command. Reaches into pocket. Retrieves same flat object. Key card. Presses it to exit. Door opens.

He goes.

"While it's just the two of us here, I'd like to ask you some basic questions, if that's alright," Doctor says. "We can take a few moments to get to know each other a little better. That sounds like a good use of our time. For starters, how is your pain? Any better, James?"

Better. *Much* better. Still there. Brain still throbs. Jaw aches. Eyes burn. But, duller. Better.

"Y…" Word doesn't come out.

Doctor understands. "Why don't you hold up your fingers for me? 10 is the most pain you've ever experienced in your life," holds up both hands, "and none is no pain at all." Balls them into fists. "For perspective, let's say five is a hangover as a point of reference." Considers his example. "Have you ever had a hangover, James?"

Think so? Probably…?

Nod anyway. Room spins faster. Eyes won't track. Shut lids. Open again. Watch Doctor.

"Good, then we understand each other, I believe. Hold up your fingers for me, James. How much pain are you experiencing right now?"

Arm heavy like head was. Hard to lift off chest. Only rises a small distance. Fingers move, though. Raise one… two… three… four. Stop.

"Four fingers, James? Is that right?"

Nod.

"And, that's less than before?"

Try to speak. No words come out. Nod again.

"While I'm sorry that you're still in pain, I'm very glad to hear that, James. Since it's working, Andrew and I can give you additional medication in a little while if you would like. For now, I need to learn a bit more about you first."

Doctor reaches under chair. Grabs clipboard. Digs pen out of shirt pocket. Clicks. Writes something on paper clipped to it.

"I'm going to label this patient record as 'James' for the time being. I'll change it when we know more. That will be exciting, won't it? To know your real name. I'm quite looking forward to it."

Nod. Focus on Doctor's face. Fight off vertigo.

Happy with this. He smiles.

"It's a long shot, I know, but do you have any idea how old you are, James? A rough estimate would suffice."

Old... age. *Number? Not there.* Missing like name.

Shake head.

"That's alright. I can approximate for now. Judging by your appearance, I'll write down twenty-six with a question mark. We'll circle back to it later." Doctor taps back of pen against board. "I suppose a medical history is out of the question. While expected, that is unfortunate. We'll have to be careful about potential allergies." Ink on his fingers. Rubs chin. Leaves blue mark. "Have you remembered anything at all, James? Does anything sound familiar? We'd like to determine where you live and whether you have close friends or relatives."

How?

Buzzing intensifies. Light flickers again. Doctor scowls at it. Stands. Taps fixture. Blinking stops. Sits back down.

"Anything might be relevant at this stage, James. Things you remember tasting or smelling. Places that stand out. Sounds you like or dislike. Foods you're craving. What comes to mind?"

Foods... places... sounds... smells...

Think hard. Focus. Try to remember. Something. Anything.

There's something in back of mind. But, it's broken. Bits and pieces. A memory. Not whole. Gibberish.

Fragments surface.

Dark room. Couch. Television. Greasy, square box.

"Pizza." This word comes out. Not lost like other ones.

Doctor's eyes widen in surprise. Face tips up. Locks onto information. "That's a great start, James. What about pizza? Do you like pizza?"

Stomach growls. Mouth waters.

"Y…" Stuck again. Clear throat. "Yes."

"Good!" Doctor scribbles on paper. Looks at me again. "Pizza is delicious, isn't it? But, there are so many different kinds, aren't there? I have to wonder, what do you like on your pizza, James?"

Close eyes. Try to answer. Let mind drift. Imagine.

Feel it on my tongue. Between my teeth. Thick. Hot. Salty. Gooey.

"Cheese."

"Ah, yes. That sounds wonderful. Just cheese, James? Anything else?"

Nod head again. "S… sausage."

"Mmm, that does sound appetizing. I haven't had pizza for quite some time. That's a shame. Perhaps, such a situation should be rectified. Tell me, though. Where do you get your pizza from, James? Do you remember? I might like to order some from there, too."

Where? *Somewhere.* Has to come from somewhere. Doesn't just appear.

Faint recollection of answering door. Young man. Red uniform. Hat. White letters. Design on box. Takes money. Wanders off.

"Mouse."

"Mouse?" Doctor repeats, confused. "Mouse…" He thinks. Pushes glasses up nose. Taps pen on board again. Stares at wall for moment. Then, looks into eyes. "Is there a mouse on the pizza box, James?"

Nod. Nod. Nod. Nod. "Yes!" Voice cracks. Cough. Hurts chest. Ribs. "Yes. M… mouse! Yes!"

"I'm so glad to hear that, James!" Doctor smiles. Whole face stretches. Eyes light up. Happy. Excited. Scribbles again. "Did you know that most people order food from restaurants close to their homes? If this is true of you as well, I may be able to track down a nearby pizza parlor with a mouse on the box. It's not a mascot one would often expect to find at such an establishment, and that gives us an advantage. I'll get started on that right away, as soon as Andrew brings you water, okay?"

Worn out. Too much thinking. Pillow too comfortable. So tired. Body wants me to sleep. Lids try to close.

Door opens. Andrew comes back. Gives Doctor water and small, rectangular package. Doctor opens lid, places bottle in hand. Plastic crinkles. Crackers in other hand now.

"Please, James. Try to drink some water and eat. It isn't much, but your body needs something. It will help." Gestures toward hands. "I don't know when you last had food. Can you do that for me? Hydrate? Enjoy a quick snack?"

Nod head. "H…"

"Help?"

Nod again.

Doctor gently lifts arm. Tips water into mouth.

Too much at first. Choke.

"Oh, I'm sorry, James." Doctor lowers limb.

Sputter. Breathe.

"Would you like some more?" Doctor raises arm again.

Ready this time. Drink. Drink fast. Drink and drink and drink and drink and drink... never enough.

Water gone. Only drops left.

Doctor takes empty bottle away. Hands to Andrew.

"Thank you so much, James. That was very good. Now, if you wouldn't mind trying the crackers, too..."

Lift other arm myself. Hard, but manage.

Crackers salty. Dry. Stick to roof of mouth.

Swallow hard. Chew until gone.

Doctor brushes crumbs off chest and neck. Pats my shoulder. Stands and takes chair with him. Walks to door.

"I won't give you a sedative, as I promised, but I truly believe you should close your eyes and rest a while. No harm will come to you under my watch. In fact, I'll have Andrew wait just outside your door."

Blink slowly. Losing battle with consciousness.

"You're going to get through this, James," Doctor adds. Voice sad but hopeful. "Andrew and I will make sure of it."

Andrew opens door again.

"I'm going to find that pizza place, James. Mark my words."

Eyes shut. Refuse to open. Everything black.

Door closes.

I'm already gone.

CHAPTER 5

THEN

"YOUR FRIEND, HUH?" THE BARTENDER ASKS, DRAWING CLOSER TO Braxton and I. Annoyance is written all over her face, but she hides it behind a customer service smile, showing off her perfectly straight white teeth. Another patron a few stools away tries to flag her down as she passes. Throwing up her palm, she silences him quickly. Her eyes are glued to Braxton. "Not you? That's so sad." Pretending to pout, she grinds her fist into her eye like a small child trying to hide their tears. "Although I have to say, it's awfully brave of you to admit you've got a micro. Most guys shy away from it, but you own it. Brava."

Braxton's jaw drops in surprise. Women don't speak to him like this. He's good-looking enough, and his family's got money. There's always someone ready to follow him home. The bartender doesn't care. I'm sure she's dealt with plenty of pricks like him tonight.

He openly ogles the blonde, who wipes her hands on a small white apron draped over the front of her jeans. A pack of cigarettes and a lighter peek out of one of the pockets. Noticing, she tucks them back in, then turns to me.

"It seems your friend has lost the ability to speak, so you'll have to place your order for yourself. Think you can handle it, honey?" Overhead, the colored bulbs switch to magenta, casting her blue uniform top into an odd shade of purple. Her golden eyes flash an orange so deep, it's almost red.

Before Braxton has a chance to run his mouth again, I reach over and shut it. His teeth click. "Don't mind him. He doesn't think before he says things. Never has."

"Pity," she answers. Sarcasm drips from her words. "Money doesn't buy couth." Her head tilts to the side, and her blonde ponytail swings. The bartender places her hands on the sticky wood and leans closer to me. A gold name tag pinned to her ample chest glints. In crisp, blocky letters, it reads: Allison. "So, what's your poison?"

"Never been here before," I tell her. "Don't even know what you've got."

"Anything." She reaches over the bar and retrieves a laminated menu. A strip of pale flesh appears between the waistband of her ripped jeans and her form-fitting tee. An all-black tattoo of a pocket watch and chain, partially obscured by her apron, wraps around the plush of her contoured, full hips. It's visible for only an instant before she tosses the menu to me. "Shots, drafts, martinis… whatever gets you off."

"Pretty bartenders, especially ones who are way out of his league." It seems Braxton has found his voice again. "Got one of those on tap?"

Allison shakes her head with contempt. "Neither of you could handle the house special. It comes with a kick." She pushes herself away from the bar and, not giving us a second thought, starts back toward the other customer.

"You sure about that?" Braxton calls after her. I jab him in the ribs, but he only laughs.

Allison stops abruptly and turns on her heel. For a second, she considers him. Her gorgeous eyes trail from his slicked-back hair down to his stomach and back up again. Finding nothing to her taste, the bartender's mouth presses into a thin line. She licks her lips and scoffs. "Darling, I eat guys like you for dinner."

"Not breakfast?" I ask, curious. "Isn't that the saying?"

She looks at me and winks. "Of course not. They never last until the morning." I'm left speechless as Allison snatches a bottle of Gin and a shot glass from a nearby shelf. "Call me when you're ready to drink."

CHAPTER 6

THEN

BRAXTON MASSAGES MY SHOULDERS WITH FAR TOO MUCH FORCE, SHAKING me from side to side. Rather than relieve pain, this is meant to cause discomfort. His thumbs drive into my muscle, leaving behind small bruises. He does this all the time. It's his version of a psych-up, a pep talk with no words.

"You're such a prick." I shake him off and glare at him.

Braxton steps back and feigns hurt, face falling. "Am not." He unbuttons his cuffs and rolls up his sleeves, securing them just below the elbow.

"Fine, a cockblock."

Braxton frowns. "Who, me?" He shakes his head. "Never. I'm an MVP."

"What do you call that, then?" I ask, gesturing toward Allison. The bartender's back is turned to us, giving me an exquisite view of her heart-shaped ass. Ice batters against the edge of the cocktail shaker in her hand as she mixes up someone's martini. She tips it over the glass and fills it to the brim.

Begrudgingly, I have to admit he did pick a gorgeous woman. There's no doubt about that.

Braxton watches her for a moment, then shrugs. "Tactical aid?"

"Fuck you," I say, tearing my eyes away from Allison. I should be nicer to Braxton, but I'm irritated. His attempts to drag me from my sorrows are only making things worse. Now, there's another woman I can't have. "I didn't even want to go out tonight."

"You *never* want to go out," he replies. "Without me, you'd hole yourself up in your apartment and shrivel like a mummy." Bracing his back against the bar, he surveys the dance floor. "The only way anyone would know you'd died is by the smell. I'm doing you a favor, man."

"How?" Irritation quickly gives way to anger. "You dragged me out here," I gripe. "Told me to get laid. Insisted that I try to score with her, then tanked the game. This is bullshit."

He doesn't respond to my complaints. Instead, Braxton ignores me and zeroes in on a brunette in the far corner. She's trying to maneuver around the other dancers, but she's three sheets to the wind, unsteady on her feet. The drink in her hand sloshes over the side of her cup when she wobbles. The drunk woman barely manages to stay upright by grabbing onto a stranger for support. Slowly, she makes her way to the wall and collapses against it.

"Whatever. You acted like a moron." I drag my eyes back to Allison, who couldn't care less about my existence. She hauls a huge bucket of ice over to a bin under the counter. The muscles in her arms flex, but she doesn't strain. The activity barely fazes her. Water dribbles from the container as she pours the contents into the chest, refilling it, and slams the lid.

Despite myself, I find this stupidly attractive. I shouldn't, but I guess it has been a minute since my last go around. Plus, Celeste never did manual labor. She was too afraid to break a nail or mess up her clothes. Something tells me Allison doesn't have the same qualms. After spending years with a "pick-me" girl who fancied herself a princess, the bartender's quick wit, attitude, and strength are incredibly alluring.

Turning away, I try not to notice how she swishes her hips when she walks. Or the way she bites her lip when she concentrates. Or the way she looks up at customers through thick, dark eyeliner and long lashes.

Already, my zipper strains against the growing bulge in my jeans. *Shit. Now I'm hard.* And, I have only myself to blame.

It doesn't matter, though. Braxton's already ruined the *infinitesimal* chance I may have had to win her over. After his antics, if I try to pick her up, I'll look like a fool. I already do. There's not a snowball's chance in hell I can get Allison into my bed.

Stop thinking about getting laid. It's not happening.

"She wants nothing to do with us now." I hurl my words at Braxton like an accusation. He doesn't notice when I shift on the stool and tug on my jeans to relieve the pressure on my dick, or maybe he pretends not to notice.

I'm way too goddamn sober for this.

That's a situation I can rectify, at least. I'd be better off drinking myself into oblivion like the chick Braxton can't take his eyes off of. It'll hurt like hell tomorrow, but tonight will disappear. I don't want to remember any of this.

Time to wipe my memories.

Tilting the menu, I make a futile attempt to read it. Across the top, looping cursive letters spell out: The Rabbit Hole. That must be the club's name. Next to it, there's a line sketch of a hare sitting on its hind legs. But, that's all I can see. The words below it are too small, and the strobes flashing behind me cast spotty glare on the lamination. Even squinting, I can't make out a thing.

"Not us," Braxton says as I struggle, splitting his attention between me and the drunk woman. One of her thin tank top straps has slipped off her shoulder. She struggles to put it back in place, then gives up when it falls again. His focus never leaves her, but he conspiratorially tilts his head closer to mine. "She wants nothing to do with *me*. *You*, on the other hand, have a chance to come out of this as a hero."

Dropping the menu, I rub my eyes, blinking away the beginnings of a headache. "What?"

He nods. "You heard me. When she comes back here, tell me off."

"What's that supposed to do?"

"I'm the jerk. Make me the villain. I'll say something…" He pauses as the brunette slides all the way down to the floor, sipping her drink. Her tiny skirt rides up her thighs. If it weren't for her fishnets, we'd be able to see everything. "Dickish. Tell me off, and she'll be putty in your hands."

"Are you fucking serious?" I demand.

"As the grave," he says with a smirk. "Besides, I think I might have found my own date."

The drunk woman tosses her empty plastic cup into the trash can beside her. She tries to stand, but can't find her footing.

"Hurry up already. I have places to be." Braxton pops a few of the buttons running down his chest. "She," he nods toward the wasted girl, "needs a friend."

"You're shameless," I tell him, but Braxton's already turning back to the counter and raising his hand to get Allison's attention. She ignores him.

"Life's not worth living if you regret things," he says simply. "When she comes over here, order your drink so I can make myself scarce."

"We've been here all of fifteen minutes. So, what? You forced me to go out just so you could abandon me? Fuck, that's shady," I bitch.

"Is not," he retorts. "Nobody likes a third wheel. I disappear, you get laid. I stay, you don't. Easy as that."

I groan and tip my head toward his prize. "Let her sober up a bit first before you try to take her home."

"Jesus, I'm not a monster." Braxton's lip curls in disgust.

"Tonight, you could have fooled me."

"I know about consent, man. Yes means yes. No means no. Drunk means… well, wait about thirty minutes and make sure she remembers her name first." He laughs and lifts my arm, waving it in the air like a flag.

Allison sees it, rolls her eyes, and holds up her finger, the universal gesture for, "hold your fucking horses." She separates a stack of bills into their respective slots and passes a customer their change. Bumping the register shut with her hip, she closes the distance between us.

"What can I do for you?" the bartender asks impatiently. Are you going to buy something this time? I'm busy." Her voice is terse.

"Customer service in this place is absolute shit," Braxton replies without missing a beat. "Hope your bedside manner is better, sweetheart."

"*Sweetheart*?" Allison repeats. "Open your mouth again, and I'll stick my foot so far up your ass, you'll taste my sneakers."

Alright, fine. Once again, we'll do things his way. The opening doesn't get any bigger than this.

"Be nice to me, and I've got a tip for you." Braxton smirks.

"Lay off," I say, standing up and shoving my friend away. "What's wrong with you?" It's supposed to be an act, but part of me really wanted to do it. I wind up pushing him harder than I'd meant to.

"What's wrong with *me*?" Braxton plays along, stumbling backward and jostling one of the stray dancers who lingers by the bar. The woman is clearly irritated by the disruption, but he doesn't say anything to fix the issue. "What's wrong with *you*? God, nobody can take a joke these days."

"Leave her alone, Braxton. She's not interested. Why don't you go find something better to do?" Leveling my glare on him, I flex my hands, then bunch them into fists, ready to come to her defense.

Why am I so angry? And, over someone I don't know?

"Whatever." He grumbles indecipherably and shoves me back onto my stool. "Good luck getting home tonight, asshole." Braxton shifts his gaze to the bartender and raises an eyebrow. "And, fuck you too, *sweetheart.*"

Allison's eyes narrow as Braxton crosses the dance floor and disappears.

CHAPTER 7
NOW

DIDN'T MEAN TO SLEEP.

Wake up to empty room. Startle. Gasp for air.

Heart pounds in chest. Drenched in sweat. Clammy. Cold.

Doctor gone. Andrew, too.

Away for long time. Too long.

Left me alone.

Thought that would be better. No one close. No one to torture. No more pain. Only self.

Wrong. Wrong. So wrong. So fucking wrong.

Can't focus. Eyes burn. World blurs.

Paranoia…

Sleep comes. Then, goes. Then, comes again.

Tempts. Eludes. Taunts.

Sucks me in. Chews me up. Spits me out.

Plagued by nightmares. Bits and pieces. Jagged shards. Too real, yet somehow impossible.

Begin nice enough. Same things. Neon lights. Plush bedding. Rose petals.

Blue. Unnatural. Odd.

Dreams suddenly shift.

Instinctual horror. Repulsion. Of what? Don't know.

See flashes. Blood. So much blood. Drip… drip… dripping onto floor.

Her face. Hovering above. Watching. Shifting.

Her eyes. Deep, unnatural crimson. Her nails. Teeth. Tongue.

Terrified to rest. Afraid to wake. Struggle to keep calm. To decipher truth.

Still exhausted. Can't focus. Lids heavy like stone. Keep trying to close.

Won't let them. Fighting so hard. Losing battle.

Losing everything.

Wanted Doctor and guard to leave. Wish they would come back now. Make it stop. Fix me.

Trust them? Not sure. *Maybe?* Maybe not…

Doctor seems kind. Doesn't push. Says nice things. Eases the pain.

Says he wants to help. Make it better. To protect.

Not like her. She wants to maim. To torture. Devour.

No.

Don't want that. Need to keep away. To hide. Run.

Somewhere nearby, clock ticks. Toks. Tiks. Toks. Sound hypnotizing.

Could be seconds. Minutes. Hours. Days…

Lose track.

Lights buzz. So loud…

Wasps still in fixtures. Creep into my brain. Crawl on my skin. Stinging, biting, gnawing.

It hurts. It itches. Want to swat them away.

Can't scratch. Nails like knives. Barely a touch, skin slices. Shreds. Carves into deep trenches. Ribbons.

Sight makes me recoil. Want to vomit.

Do it anyway. Can't resist, either. Must pull them out. The bugs. Get them off of me. Dig and dig and dig.

Can't find them.

Not there? In my mind? Invisible? Incurable torment.

Only more blood.

Not in dreams. The nightmares. Imagined.

No, here and now. In reality.

Drip… drip… drip…

Runs down forearms. Trails across wrists. Bright contrast against purple and blue bruises. Stains my fingers. Dyes the ridges. Shocking ruby swirls.

Soaks into mattress. Deep scarlet.

Falls to floor in puddles. Spreads. Smears.

Drip. Drip. Plunking sound pierces silence. Deafening. All consuming.

Little crimson beads. Glistening. Innocent drops. Dainty, round circles.

So red, so red, so very red. Red. Red.

Stare in fascination. Fixate. Morbid curiosity.

Then, something new.

Eyes stare back from mess I've made. From deep within puddles.

Portals.

Body freezes. Petrifies. Becomes statue.

Heart stops. Stutters. Lurches.

It's her. She's watching. She knows.

Found me. Even here. Sees me. Knows where I am. Where to go.

Not safe. Not safe. Not safe. Not safe.

Never was. Definitely not anymore.

Have to go. Get away. Out of time. Do it now!

"Help!" I scream. "Help! Help me..." Voice becomes wail. "Help... Please! Please, help!"

Click from the door. Doctor flies in. Rushes to side. Tries to aid.

Andrew only steps behind. Stops and stares at mess. Eyes wide. Mouth open.

Afraid? Surprised?

Provoked?

Not good. *No, no, no, no, no...*

Reaches for Doctor. Doctor moves away. Guard's hand falls short. Drops back to side.

"James," Doctor says. "Can you hear me, James?"

On the floor.

How? Not in the bed. Was in bed. *What happened? Fell?*

Dreamed it all?

No.

Tile wet. Sticky like glue. Clings to cheek. Coats face in gore.

"I'm sorry to have been gone for so long," Doctor adds. "Someone should have checked in on you. This was a grave oversight." Pointed glance at Andrew. "It will be dealt with. I'm so sorry, James. Words cannot express my regrets. But, I'm here now. I'm ready to help."

Don't move. Stay perfectly still. Try to fill in the gaps... the holes...

Andrew stares. Eyes fixed on me. Shoulders tight. Rigid. Locked. Hand on baton.

Watches. Waits. Readies.

For what?

Doctor drops to knees. Hands on the floor. Ignores mess. Lies down beside me. Face near mine. Sad. Very, very sad. Concerned.

Why?

"You're bleeding, James. The medication we've given you can cause pruritus. Itching. I've never known it to provoke such a severe reaction, or I would have certainly been monitoring you much more closely. You've scratched yourself rather badly, I'm afraid."

Scratched? Yes. To find them. The bugs.

"Will you let me help you, James?"

"Help," I whisper. Echo Doctor's words. A cry. A plea. So quiet. Barely hear it.

Doctor smiles. "Yes, help. I'd like to help you with your bleeding. We should clean up these injuries and bandage them as soon as possible, James. Open wounds can cause infection, especially in hospitals. That's the last thing you want, I assure you. You've got quite enough on your plate right as it is."

"Help..." Repeat again.

Doctor breathes deep. "Andrew, please get the nurse. We'll need supplies right away."

Andrew looks at Doctor. At me. At puddles. Swallows. Weighs options.

Blood. So much blood. Oceans of it. Enough to paint the tile.

Like before.

Where? Wherever she was...

Doctor clears throat. Subtle command.

"Yes, Dr. Barrows," Andrew agrees. Then, activates exit. Door shuts behind him. He fades from view.

Doctor remains. Stays with me. Reaches out. Not in anger. Tentatively. Respectfully.

Stills my hand. Was digging at floor. Hadn't noticed.

Examine limb. Fingernails shredded. Chipped. Torn.

Doctor holds in place. Gentlest touch.

"It's going to be alright, James." Tips head compassionately with other hand. Makes me look at him. "I know it doesn't feel that way right now, but it will. You're not alone, even when I'm not in this room. Everyone in this hospital is on your side. We're here with you. Never far."

Blink sluggishly. Lost in adrenaline. In erratic beat of heart.

"How about we get you back in bed?" Doctor asks. "That would be much more comfortable, yes?"

Nod. "Bed."

"Good, James. Very good. Your comfort is important. Let's do that, then." Light squeeze. "I'm going to sit up. Is that alright?"

"Up," I parrot.

"Okay. I'll do it slowly so you can clearly see my movements. Please, let me know if you need me to pause or to stop anything. You're in control. Just keep your eyes with me, James. Follow me. Watch what I'm doing. Remember, I mean you no harm."

Doctor adjusts. Pushes up onto elbows. Shifts until sits on knees. Still holds my hand. Rubs back of it with thumb. Comforting. Calming.

Waits a moment.

"Can you sit up with me, James?" he wonders. Smiles. Still sad. Less obvious. Deep in his eyes now. "I feel rather silly sitting on the floor on my own, truth be told."

Mirror Doctor's transition. Hard. Body trembles too much.

Use arms for leverage. Ripping sound. Wet squelch. Cheek peels off tile. Strangely tacky. Flaky. Cold.

Lips coated with iron.

Gag. Tastes familiar. *Tastes wrong.*

Wrong...

"Thank you for joining me, James. That was difficult, I'm sure. But, seeing you strong makes me feel strong, too. Things are much easier if we do them together, don't you think?"

Nod.

"Yes, I agree. Now, I'd like to move to the mattress. Will you join me there, as well?"

"Mattress," I say. Doctor likes answer. That I spoke. "Bed," I add.

"Alright. I'll go first, just as I did before, then you can follow."

Doctor stands. Offers other hand. Finds my fingers. Slick. Brown now. Rusty.

"It's like a game, isn't it? Follow the leader. We used to play it as children, didn't we?"

Follow the leader. The pied piper.

Kidnapper.

Follow where? Down... down somewhere. Down the hall? No, not hall. Another word. A phrase. On the tip of tongue.

Into the darkness. The shadows. The void. Hiding from the dawn.

Doctor moves grip up arm. Steadies me as I rise. Finds hold in armpit. Light tug. Rights my feeble form.

"You're doing so well, James," Doctor reassures. Real smile. Pulls me to bed. Springs creak. Muted. "We will get you cleaned up as soon as Andrew returns. I'll bandage these wounds, and we'll lay you back down on another clean pillow. How does that sound?"

Lay down. Down. Down…

Falling.

So confused. Nothing makes sense.

Safe. Safe. Safe… Remind self. *Doctor here. Doctor is kind.*

"Would you like to know what I've learned so far, James? That's why I was gone. I was researching the mouse we discussed. The one from the pizza box."

Doctor waits for answer. Doesn't look at me. Just sits. Lets me think. Mull over.

"Yes."

Smiles. Happy. Very, very happy. Sadness gone. Likes my words. My voice. "There's a lovely little pizzeria uptown called The DoorMouse. They have a mouse on their pizza boxes. Funny things, mice. They do love cheese. That would make sense, now wouldn't it?"

Mice. Cheese. Twitchy nose. Fur. Soft. Small.

"Yes."

"As it happens, they have three locations nearby, but *only* three. This is helpful information, James. The DoorMouse Pizzeria isn't a national chain. I'm going to call and ask about men who look like you and pizza orders that fit the food you described. Perhaps, with any luck, I can determine where you live, maybe even your name. We're making progress. Progress is good."

Andrew comes back. This time, not alone. Brings Nurse.

Woman trails behind with metal cart. Wheels groan. Door shuts.

Seals us in.

She's scared. Shaking. Stays back. Stares.

"Ah, Marianne. Thank you for your assistance. It seems James here has injured himself. Let's patch him up. We can't have a patient in distress. He deserves comfort and rest."

Nurse Marianne swallows. Big gulp. Falters.

"Quickly, now. I'm sure this hurts," Doctor orders.

Nurse grabs bandages. Bottle of liquid. Something sharp.

A needle.

Sedative?

Danger. Wants to subdue me. Knock me out!

Terror rises uncontrollably. Spurs body into action. Brings strength back to legs and arms.

"No!" I roar. Volume shocks my senses.

Lose hold over self.

Shove doctor away. Leap from bed. Charge at Nurse. Dodge Andrew. Bolt for door.

Have to get out. To fight. To survive.

No needles. No more medication. No more sleep. Nightmares. Thrall.

Nurse collapses at my touch. Screams in surprise and fear. Head smacks wall — hard. Body hits floor. Drops everything she holds.

Bandages unroll. Skitter along tile. Needle flies across room. Vanishes under bed.

She scoots away. Moves fast. Trembles. Cries from shock.

Andrew snatches shoulders. Incredibly strong. Throws me down. Away from Nurse. Away from Doctor, too.

Splitting pain. In head. In joints. Ribs. Spine.

Room spins. He straddles chest. Weighs me down. Squeezes too tight. Too tight. Too…

Can't breathe. *Suffocating.*

Black specks flood eyes. Steal my vision. Darkness comes.

Gasp for air. Grab for wrists. Scratch at hold. Claw at face. Kick. Jerk.

Not working. Nothing… nothing working.

"Enough!" Doctor yells. Hear his voice from far away. "Let go of him this instant, Andrew. He's only frightened. He didn't mean to hurt anyone."

"This man is dangerous, Doctor Barrows." Andrew grunts. Face purple. Holds ground. Relaxes grip, but only slightly. Not enough. Can't move. Can't escape.

"So are you in certain circumstances, this being one of them. Let him go, Andrew. This patient is in our care, and I will not see you harm him. I've given you an order. Do what I say." Doctor calm. Not same calm as before. Different. Controlled. "Now."

Andrew releases throat. Adjusts weight. Widens legs. Leans back.

Still pinned to ground, but air comes. Sputter. Neck throbs. Chest aches. Head pounds.

"Help," I whimper. Pathetic. "Doctor, help…"

Panic. Pain. Rage. Defeat. Too many emotions war.

Doctor comes closer. Andrew stands. Puts hands up. Backs away. Angry.

Doctor bends down. Frowns. Clasps shoulder. "We're trying, James. We just don't know how."

CHAPTER 8

THEN

BRAXTON'S FORM MERGES WITH THE THRONG OF WRITHING BODIES AS THE DJ mixes one song into the next. The floor vibrates under my feet, brought to life by the thrumming bass. Overhead, the lights shift, pulsating like breath.

Allison's narrowed eyes remain fixed on Braxton until he's completely gone. She taps her unmanicured fingernails against the bar, matching the beat. Jaw set in a hard line, a not-so-subtle threat of violence lingers in her expression. If I didn't know better, I'd say he's lucky she didn't lean across the counter and throttle him then and there.

Finally, she turns her gaze back to me. Her eyes are cold, assessing.

"Order a drink or get the hell away from my bar," she commands. "I don't have time for you or your dickhead friend. Other people are waiting."

She's right about that. As if on cue, one of the customers knocks back a shot and slams his empty shot glass onto the counter with a bang. He waves for Allison and calls, "Refill!"

"You'll get your refill when you hand over your keys, Wayne!" she snaps.

"Aw, come on," the man complains. "Don't be like that."

Allison turns her head to him and, letting go of the bar, makes an obscene gesture.

"I'm not like him," I say before she can walk away. "Braxton."

"You certainly keep pleasant company," she retorts, dragging her attention back to me.

She's got me there.

"He's not always this bad." But, even I know my words are flimsy. He's not usually much better, either. Besides, why would she care? He's just an arrogant man who wandered into the club and started acting like he owns the place. "That's no excuse," I tell her. "He won't apologize, so I will. I'm sorry he behaved that way. You deserve better."

Allison scoffs. "I don't need your apologies or your knight-in-shining-armor routine. Trust me, I've seen it before. You're all the same."

Well, there goes Braxton's scheme. Not that I'd put much stock in it to begin with. It's just easier to do what he wants than to argue with him.

That makes me sound like a sheep. And, it doesn't only apply to Braxton. Am I really just letting people shepherd me from one choice to the next without ever making my own? *Probably.* Maybe that's why Celeste is gone. *I've always been a lamb on my way to the fucking slaughter…*

"He's trying to help," I admit, embarrassed. "It's misguided. Good intentions, poor execution."

Wayne shoves his shot glass in Allison's direction. Without looking, she plucks it off the sticky wood and tosses it into a dish bin under the bar.

Allison leans onto her forearms, though somehow, her posture remains rigid. Those appraising eyes land on me again. She studies me like a specimen under a microscope. If I wasn't so distracted, I might be a little irritated. As it stands, the thin fabric of her shirt strains against her breasts

She's not wearing a bra, I notice. It takes everything I have not to stare at her cleavage. The peaks of her nipples are clearly visible beneath the cotton. If it wasn't so dark, I could probably see the exact shade of pink contrasting against her alabaster skin. My thoughts drift to fantasies of caressing them between my lips. I swallow hard.

From far away, the bartender was attractive. Up close, Allison is exquisite. She knows it, too. Owns it. Flaunts it.

"Help with what?" she probes.

"You don't need my apologies, and I don't need your pity," I reply, avoiding the question. I'm not the kind of guy who cries into his beer-stained napkin and seeks solace in strangers.

Her head tilts to the side in challenge.

"Shit happens. Braxton's answer for every setback is a stiff drink and loose women."

For the first time tonight, Allison chuckles, catching me off guard. A ghost of a genuine smile flits across her features. Her gorgeous golden eyes darken with a hint of mischief. "Not yours?"

"No. I prefer solitude."

That's not exactly true, but I'd rather sit in my empty apartment and play my games than deal with the unnecessary judgment. All anyone seems to do these days is look at me like an injured bird. My mother. My friends. Hell, even my boss. It sucks.

At least Braxton was upfront. Everyone else tries to hide it, but it's so damn obvious.

Feigning detachment, I lift the menu and pretend to read it.

Allison sees right through me. She straightens up, snatches the glossy page, and fans herself with it. "Bullshit."

"Whatever."

Trying not to come across as pathetic, I shift my focus back to the dance floor and attempt to find Braxton. It doesn't take long. He emerges from the crowd and beelines for the sloshed brunette. I watch as he stoops to her level and offers her his hand.

Dazed, she takes it and allows him to pull her onto her unsteady feet. She sways in his grip but manages to remain standing. Braxton wraps one arm around her waist and uses the other to point to the bathroom, then mimes splashing water on his face.

"If you prefer your own company so much, why do you hang out with a guy like him?" Allison asks, refusing to let it go.

"Because there's no one else waiting for me." The admission stings.

"I don't buy it."

"Look," I say, hoping to deflect the conversation, "it doesn't matter what you think." She shakes her head, which is irrationally frustrating. "You're hot, sure," I continue. "That doesn't mean I owe you my life story."

My curt response takes Allison aback. I hadn't meant to be so harsh. I don't want to talk about Celeste. It's as simple as that.

"I didn't ask for your biography, asshole," she says. "I was being nice. Just thought I'd give you a chance to redeem yourself. I like broken men. If you want to suffer alone, that's your choice."

Now, it's my turn to be surprised. "Excuse me?"

She smirks. "I like broken men. I said what I said."

"I'm not fucking broken." This time, I mean for my answer to sound surly. I *am* broken, but I don't have to tell her that. Unfortunately, rather than tough, I come across as defensive. So, I tack on, "I had a fiancée, and now I don't. There, happy?"

Allison considers this. "Your fault or hers?"

"Hers. She left."

"Why?"

Her question hangs in the air. I get the sense that this is a pivotal moment. Up until now, Allison hadn't given me the time of day.

I weigh my options. I could lie, tell her I don't know. Or, I could tell the truth. Admit she had an affair.

The bartender waits for me to answer without interrupting.

Settling on honesty, I say, "She went back to her ex."

"That blows," she offers. There's no judgment on her face. No pity. Only interest.

"Yeah."

The song changes again. Braxton's "date" emerges from the restroom with her shoes dangling from her hand. Wet strands of hair stick to the brunette's cheeks. He swipes them away and tucks them behind her ear before leading her to a vacant corner to chat.

"You want to get smashed for fun or to forget?" Allison asks, tapping the menu in her hands and stealing my attention away from the pair.

"Is there a difference?"

"Oh, yeah." Allison raises one eyebrow and bites her lip. The skin blossoms red between her teeth.

God, I want to bite that lip for her.

Woah, where did that come from?

"I can mix up something to make you larger than life if you want. Get you out on that dance floor making a fool of yourself. Or, I can get you something to make you smaller. Make you forget your fiancée ever existed. Make you a blip on the radar."

What do I want? I mull this over for a moment. I want things to be easier. Less painful. I want to be someone else. Not a "broken man."

So, there it is. The only option. "I want to forget."

Allison offers me a knowing look and wanders over to the liquor shelf. She picks up a martini glass, wets the rim, and dips it into a tray of white powder. I expect her to mix up a margarita, albeit in the wrong cup, but she grabs several different bottles instead. When she's finished, the concoction is as blue as her t-shirt. She garnishes the drink with a gummy worm and a maraschino cherry.

As she carries it over to my seat, Allison takes a sip. The powder lining the rim smudges, and she licks it off her lips. Before slipping a cocktail napkin beneath the glass, she pulls a pen out of her apron pocket and scrawls something on the paper. Without spilling a drop, she sets the drink in front of me and smiles.

"Down the hatch," she says. "I'll start you a tab. And by the way, my bedside manner is to die for. I fuck hard and fast like a rabbit."

Her unexpected candor makes my cock jump. I swallow.

The bartender wanders her way over to Wayne and holds out her hand.

When the spotlight flares, I'm able to read the words "Drink Me" written in thick blue letters on the edge of the napkin. The blatant command makes me laugh.

Allison watches me as I raise the glass, offering a silent "cheers." She winks, mimics me by shaking Wayne's keys in the air, and slides the register drawer open. Then, she locks them inside and turns her back.

CHAPTER 9

THEN

WHICHEVER LIQUORS ALLISON COMBINED, SHE DISTRIBUTED WITH A HEAVY hand. By no means am I an amateur in the mixed drink department, and yet, the first swallow steals my breath. Blazing heat sears my throat, the sensation verging on pain. My stomach roils in protest, only for a second, before the liquid settles, warming my core.

The concoction is delicious, if harsh. I've never tasted anything like it. Sweet and sour. Somehow, salty and acidic. My next inhale holds hints of tequila, sugar, and melon, but I can't make out the rest. My taste-buds are confused, and yet, I find myself wanting more.

Bracing myself this time, I take another shallow swig. The second isn't quite as bad. It coats my esophagus, stinging as it slides down. My chest tightens in a pleasant way.

Already, my lips are tingling. *Damn.*

Allison is right. A few more of these, and I'll wind up abandoning my troubles at this club. The drink is a pied piper, urging me to fade into inebriated bliss, and I want to follow. Leave Celeste and my failed engagement behind. Forget who I am. Enjoy myself for the night. Flirt with the sexy bartender. Wake up in someone else's bed in the morning.

As I'm about to raise the blue liquor to my lips again, a light tap on my shoulder makes me pause. I turn my head.

"Hey."

Braxton stands at my back. His drunken date hangs on to his hips for stability, one slender arm disappearing and reappearing from behind his frame. The other dangles at her side, still clutching her discarded shoes. He's got a shit-eating grin plastered on his face.

I've seen that look before.

"We're gonna get out of here, man." He has to strain his voice to speak over the music.

"Saw that one coming," I tell him.

He laughs. "The club is too crowded tonight. No place for privacy."

"That's never stopped you." I take another drink before adding, "Thought you were going to wait a little longer before making your move, huh?"

"Oh, come on." He groans and glances up at the clock over the bar, then back at me. "It's been, like, twenty minutes. She's fine! See?" He lets go of his hold on the still very intoxicated woman clinging to him.

Betraying the inaccuracy of his statement, the brunette hiccups and sways. He presses her body closer to his side.

Shifting my focus to her, I ask, "What's your name?"

"Dynah," the brunette replies. "It's... nicetomeetyou." These last words come out in a slurred string.

"You too," I say. I watch as she transfers her weight from one foot to the other before asking, "How are you liking my friend here?"

"He's wonderful." She trails the hand holding her heels over the buttons running down Braxton's chest and stomach. "A perfect gentleman."

A snort bursts out of me before I have a chance to stop it. Braxton smacks my arm, hard. "Seems like he's a lucky guy, too."

Dynah flashes me a lopsided grin. "Oh, he's gonna be." She winks.

"We're heading to her place," Braxton announces. "Her apartment is pretty close. A few blocks walk."

She nods, beaming with pride. "Yup. Super close. We," Dynah hiccups again, "don't even need a car."

"That's great," I tell her, "because you're in no state to drive."

"Don't be a buzzkill, asshole," Braxton complains. "Look, you remember where we parked, right?"

"Yes, Dad. In the structure." Sarcasm drips from my words.

"Ooo, can *I* call you Daddy?" Dynah giggles and snuggles up to him.

Braxton rolls his eyes and scoffs, ignoring his date's question. "Don't be a shit. I'm watching out for you. If you get drunk," he says, then rephrases, "*when* you get drunk, call a cab. Your car isn't important. I can bring you back for your ride in the morning. Got it?"

"Pinky promise." I hold my little finger out to him. Dynah reaches for it and wraps my digit with her own. Her high heels brush up against my thigh. When she lets go, I add, "Cross my heart and hope to die," in a mockingly sweet tone.

"Alright, man. Call me if you get into anything you can't handle." He follows this with a solid clap on my back. "But, wait like an hour before you do anything stupid." He winks and presses his cheek to the top of Dynah's head. "I'm a bit preoccupied."

Dynah raises her arm and buries her fingers in Braxton's jet-black hair, ruffling it. He grimaces, hating to have his perfect appearance mussed. She doesn't notice. Pressing up onto her tiptoes, she tries and fails to whisper into his ear. "Yes, you are!" she practically shouts.

"Later," Braxton says when she drops back onto her bare soles. Before leaving, he tosses a fifty onto the bar. "Keep drinking," he commands. "Have a *wonderful* evening. You better not remember it tomorrow."

"I don't plan on it," I call after him, but he's too far away to hear.

I watch as Braxton ushers his wasted prize toward the exit. Just before the three-quarter wall blocks the two of them from view, he grips a fistful of Dynah's ass. An elated squeal cuts through the din, and he hoists her over his shoulder, then carries her away, leaving me behind to fend for myself.

"Thanks for hauling me out here and ditching me, fuckface," I grumble. "I hope you can't keep it up."

Mildly irritated by his departure, I drain what's left in my glass.

I HAVEN'T ORDERED ANY MORE DRINKS, BUT LIKE MAGIC, THEY KEEP appearing in front of me. Allison brings another every time she notices my glass is empty. That's fine by me. They're surprisingly enticing. Maybe too enticing. Since I slammed the first one, I took my time with the second. Three drinks in, the room is starting to spin. *Goddamn, these are strong.*

I'll have to ask her for the recipe. On second thought, I should probably have her write it down. I doubt I'll have the capacity to retain the information. My sobriety is long gone.

Crystals of sugar cling to the rim as I set it down on my sodden paper napkin, harder than I'd intended to. It's falling to bits. Her handwritten message has become nothing but a dense cloud of ink. I can no longer decipher it, in part due to my failing vision, but mostly due to condensation and blue liquor splashes.

When I glance up, Allison's already on her way over with drink number four. This time, she carries a steaming basket alongside it.

The woman is one hell of a bartender, I'll give her that. She's been running back and forth between customers all night without missing a beat. Her efforts have caused her skin to glisten with a thin sheen of sweat. It's fucking hot, seeing her work her ass off and handle the belligerent drunks.

Celeste couldn't hold a candle to Allison if she tried. The thought creeps, unbidden, into my mind. As it does, realization dawns. *I'm glad she's fucking gone.*

That's new. Or, is it? Is that why I've been so miserable? She'd been pulling away from me for a while before I came home to our empty apartment. Engagement ring on the nightstand. Inadequate note on the bed. "I can't marry you. I'm sorry."

Liar. Fuck her.

She wasn't sorry. She was ecstatic. All it took was one look at her Instagram to see as much. Between that morning when I'd left for work and six pm, pictures of her and her ex had popped up at regular intervals. Holding hands. Kissing. Curled up under the covers, obviously nude.

I was a fool. I knew something was off, and I kept coming back for more.

I'm sick of being a glutton for punishment. There has to be something better than this. If nothing else, I need a change. Some fun. A new outlook.

Celeste has ruined enough of my life. Not tonight. She can keep the damn cat. I never liked the thing anyway. I swear, it enjoyed breaking my shit. And, she can keep the honeymoon fund. Hell, she can take whatever she wants from our time together. I don't need the reminders.

I'm moving on.

Braxton is such an asshole, but what do you know? He was right, too. He and Allison are turning out to be my salvation. I'm glad I got out of the house after all.

Speaking of moving on, the drinks have bolstered my courage. They've taken the edge off of Celeste's rejection and are spurring me on. I'm ready for another chance with the bartender.

By now, the crowd has thinned. A handful of the stools are still occupied, mostly by women clutching wine glasses. The majority of the patrons are either on the dance floor or have already left.

Wayne and I are the only two men competing for Allison's attention. I like my odds.

Allison stops in front of me and replaces my drink, then sets the basket down beside it. Straightening up, I meet her eyes and do my best to seem far less intoxicated than I am. While I'm certain she isn't fooled in the slightest, I have to try.

Wax paper lines the plastic container, surrounding a heap of fried food. Steam from the appetizer wafts into my nostrils, and I inhale. It smells delicious. A cup of creamy ranch nestles in the center. She drops a new napkin onto the counter and tosses the old one in the garbage.

My mouth waters and my stomach growls. I reach for one of the enticing little spheres, but she smacks my hand.

"Not yet, idiot. They're hot."

"What is it?" In quite the feat, I manage to keep my words spaced out appropriately, which makes me irrationally happy. I grin like a prepubescent boy who's just seen his first Playboy centerfold.

"Mushrooms," she answers. "The house special. I figured you'd want to soak up some of that booze. We have a strict rule here: No barfing at the bar. I'm not cleaning that shit up."

Making sure I got the message, she pushes the basket a little closer to me. When I nod, she reaches into her apron and withdraws the pack of cigarettes and the lighter.

Like a smartass, I pluck the napkin from under my drink and wave it in the air. "This one is blank," I complain.

"And?" she asks.

"What, no commands this time?"

Allison licks her lips and smirks. "What do you want me to write? Eat me, Big Boy?"

"Oh, yeah." I raise my eyebrows suggestively. Or, I try to, at least. "Can I?"

"Can you what?" She narrows her eyes.

"Eat you," I answer. *God, I have no shame. Shit, what kind of pickup line is that?* "Please?" I add on, hoping it comes across as dorkishly charming.

My drunken attempt at seduction fails miserably. Immediately, Allison breaks out in uncontrollable laughter. Tears stream from the corners of her eyes. She wipes them away with her sleeve.

"I'm taking a smoke break," she announces once she manages to catch her breath. Shaking her head, she plucks one of the cigarettes from the pack. The bartender tucks it behind her ear and returns the cardboard box to her apron pocket. "Behave yourself, and I'll bring you another drink when I get back."

"Yes, Miss Allison," I joke. "I'll be a *very* good boy." Forgetting her warning already, I pop an entire mushroom between my teeth.

This, I immediately regret. Scalding juice pours onto my tongue, scorching my tastebuds. With an open mouth, I chew as quickly as I can, clearing away the offending bite and swallowing most of the morsel whole.

Allison gives me a disapproving look. "Can't imagine you'll be eating much of anything if you give yourself third-degree burns, let alone my pussy, but what do I know?" She stalks away. "Impatient boychild," she mutters under her breath.

I'm too busy trying to staunch the fire in my mouth to notice which way she's gone.

CHAPTER 10

NOW

DOCTOR GIVES MORE MEDICINE. DIFFERENT THIS TIME. MEANS TO knock out.

Don't want it. Fight back. Headbutt. Lash out with arms and legs. Try to squirm across floor.

Doctor apologizes. Again, and again, and again.

Andrew holds me down. Doesn't let me get away. Halts movements. Traps arms by sides. Sticks legs between his.

Can't resist. Get away.

Needle squirts. Drips. Cloudy fluid beads on point.

Beg them not to. Plead. Cry. Whine like child.

Doesn't work. Doctor flicks tip. Splashes on cheek. Cold. Wet. Foul.

Betrayed.

Stabbing pain. Whoosh of fluid.

Doctor watches. Holds my hand. Squeezes and mutters kind words.

Andrew watches. Stoic.

Nurse takes needle. Backs away. Presses frame against door. Far from me. Afraid. Trembling.

Body stills. Stops fighting. Andrew lets go. Walks to nurse. Holds her steady.

Doctor lays on floor. Stays with me. Whispers reassurances until words run together. Become garbled.

Don't understand. Will never understand.

Eyes grow heavy. Darkness takes me.

Away, far away.

Back to her.

WAKE UP IN BED. BODY HEAVY. COLD. STIFF.

Room empty. Left me here. Alone again.

Good. Want them gone.

Traitors.

Then, whisper comes. Can't tell from where. So quiet. Like phantom.

A woman's voice.

Her voice.

Jump when realize. Heart pounds. Panic grips.

Sit up straight. On cot. Out in open.

Drop to floor. Press body into corner. Cower. Draw knees up to chest. Peer over caps and rock.

Search for her.

Need to find her. Track her. Know what she's going to do.

No one there.

Just like bugs. Invisible, yet present.

Wait and watch for eternity.

How long, really? Not sure.

Until whisper gone.

Head too heavy. Weighed down with bricks. Decide to move. Slow going.

Lift self to stand. Touch feet to icy tile. Try to balance. Keep steady.

Floor not sticky. Clean. Blood gone. Bleach smell.

Strong. Too strong. Sickening.

Nose burns. Nausea. Stomach cramps.

Bend over. Reach for bed frame. Miss once. Try again.

Fall to ground. Head swims. Manage to grab on second time. Hold it.

Cot bolted to floor. Sturdy. Steady. Lean against it. Anchor.

Beg room to stop spinning.

Mocks me.

Spins faster. Faster. Faster. Dizzy. So dizzy.

Vomit climbs. Try to push down. Stop it from coming. Doesn't matter.

Comes anyway. Explodes into mouth. Sprays from lips.

Sour taste. Acid. New puddles on laminate.

Chest squeezes. Abs clench. Body aches.

Neck swollen from Andrew's grip. Throbs where his hands were.

Ribs bruised. Arms, too. And, hips.

She calls to me again. Not a whisper. Louder. Close.

Behind me? Right there?

Turn and stare. Nothing. No one.

A ghost. Illusion. Lure. Trick.

"No, no, no…" Voice weak. Raspy. Throat raw.

"Get out!" Louder this time. Echoes off walls. "Get away! Away! Leave! Leave me alone!"

Scoot back. Use wall. Stand again.

Quaking. Eyes searching.

Where? Where?

Nowhere. Alone.

Her voice returns. Calling. Summoning. Demanding.

Sudden high pitch fills room. Ears ring. Cover with hands.

Voice only gets louder. Closer. Moves inside me. Into head.

Touch something wet. Warm. Slippery…

Look at palms. More blood. Streams from ears. Thin rivers.

"Bitch!" Screaming now. Can't help it. Losing control again. Full of anger. Terror.

Clothes too tight. Itching won't stop. More wasps. Biting. Stinging everywhere.

More bugs. Worms. Crawling under skin.

No, not worms. Maggots. Fat things. Thick. Eating from inside. Devouring inch by inch.

Clawing. Ripping. Bandages can't stop bleeding. White gauze turns red.

Dig through them. Rip off. Throw them. Carve new gashes.

Fingers stain. Dark moons under nails. Around cuticles.

"Get away!" Shrieking. Crying. "Out of my head! Get away!" Flailing.

Shut her out! Shut her out!

Eyes close. Body slams into wall. Sends me reeling.

Stumble. Fall backward. Stand. Hit wall again.

She's in veins. Burning... Tearing... Slashing... Squeezing... Ripping!

"The poison!" I hear myself say. Don't know where I am. Lost. Nothing makes sense.

Run, fall, stand, slam, fall, stand, run again. Again. Again.

"Blue poison! So blue... So sweet... Blue poison!"

Bang head on floor. Bang! BanG! BaNG! BANG!

Click. Door opens. Not alone anymore.

Doctor here. Andrew here. Mouths open. Gaping.

Pale. So pale. White like snow.

"James," Doctor murmurs. "Oh, James. Oh, I'm so sorry, James."

Keep slamming skull into tile.

Steps. Two sets. Andrew's hands on shoulders. Firm. Insistent.

Doctor's hands lift head. Gentle. Hesitant.

Doctor kneeling in front of me.

"You must calm down, James. Can you take a deep breath?"

Can't stop. Pull away from Doctor. Captures my face again.

"Breathe with me, James. Breathe with me. Remember where you are. I'm here now."

"Down the hatch." Stare up at Doctor. He shakes head. Doesn't understand. "Good boy! Good boy..." Tremble. "Swallow. Swallow it all. Drink me. Drink me! Poison!"

"He needs to be restrained," Andrew insists. "If not for your safety, then for his. Look at him, Doctor Barrows. He's going to kill himself if we don't do something."

Doctor frowns. Studies me. Crestfallen.

"Drink me," I command.

Nod at him. Doesn't answer. Try again.

"Down the hatch. Poison for you. Special. So blue. Drink me. Take it away!"

"This man has already been restrained, Andrew." Doctor rises. Pulls me up. Guides me to bed. "Look at his wrists. These are ligature marks. And, on his ankles. If we were to incapacitate him, it might only worsen his trauma."

Doctor sits down. Lays me on mattress. Fluffs pillow. Pushes hair off face.

"What does his trauma matter if he's dead?" Andrew asks.

"Blue poison," I insist. Want him to know. Need him to know. Grab Doctor's arms. Squeeze.

Not listening. Not hearing.

Keep trying. "Down the hatch. Drink me. Drink me! Blue poison…"

"Okay, James." Pulls hands away from him. Puts them in my lap. "It's going to be alright."

"Doctor?" Andrew tries.

Doctor glances away. Thinks.

Looks back at me. Full of shame. Turns to Andrew. Nods head.

Andrew relaxes. Relieved.

Not good! Not good!

"No." Try to grab again. Moves away. "No, Doctor. No!"

"I need to keep you safe." Doctor says. "Stay with him, Andrew. Keep him as calm as you can."

Not calm. Not fucking calm!

Andrew steps closer. Stands between Doctor and bed.

"I'll be right back, James."

CHAPTER 11
NOW

"UNLESS YOU HAVE ANOTHER WAY TO KEEP HIM STILL, WE'RE GOING TO have to sedate him again, Doctor Barrows."

Restraints. Cuffs. Straps everywhere. Bite into ankles. Wrists. Squeeze chest. Legs. Arms.

Noose tightening. Must escape. Break free.

Not safe. Not calm. Not okay. Not safe! Fuck!

"Blue poison!" I scream. Jerk. Tug. Stretch. Yank. "Down the hatch… the hatch… the hatch… is open. Drink me!"

New face. Blonde woman. Small. Thin. Angry. Bitter. Lips shut. Tight line. Hands on hips.

"Please, that shouldn't be necessary," Doctor answers. "As I've told Andrew, this man is afraid. It's enough that we've had to restrain him. Look at him."

"Poison. Blue poison. Onetwothreefour." Words too fast. Run together. "Four. Four. Follow. Must follow. Down the hatch."

Woman throws hands up. "While I sympathize with his madness, I cannot make the equipment do so. He either stays still, or we sedate him, or you take him back to the ward. I have other patients waiting."

"Waiting," I repeat. "Waiting. Late. Latelatelatelate. Down the hatch. Follow. Must follow. Pretty. Pretty rabbit."

Doctor turns. Looks in eye. Face scrunches. Listens.

"Poison. Blue poison. Down the hatch."

"We work with fearful patients all the time, don't we? There must be something we can do besides sedating him, Polly."

"We're out of options, Doctor Barrows. Make the call, or I will."

Woman leaves. Moves behind wall. Big window. See her beyond.

Glowing screens. Tap. Tap. Tapping keys.

"James," Doctor says. Sits on gurney. Pats arm. "Please, James. Look at me now. I know you can do it. Show me your eyes, James."

Woman keeps tapping.

Hates me. Hates doctor. Hard jaw. Teeth clenched.

"Look at me, James. I can't help you if you won't cooperate. We need to talk about what's happening. Do you understand?"

Eyes move. Away from woman. See Doctor.

Angry? Stressed?

"Follow. Down the hatch. Blue poison. Follow. Pretty rabbit. Late. Down the hatch." Words pour out of me. Can't stop them.

"Good, James," Doctor whispers. "Thank you. I know that was difficult. Polly wants to help you, as do I. After your episode in the room, we need to make sure you're safe. You hit your head on the floor multiple times, much harder than you should have. There may be fractures. You might have sustained a concussion. We won't know without this scan."

"Poison. Pretty rabbit. Late. Late. Follow."

"We are limited here, James. I know you don't like the restraints. I wish there was another way to keep you from harming yourself, but Andrew is correct. If we hadn't stopped you from engaging in self-destructive behavior, chances are you would have gravely injured yourself, or worse. Now, we face a similar situation."

Doesn't understand. Not listening. Talking too much.

Keep saying the words. Not making sense. Over and over and over and over.

"Pretty rabbit," I plead. "Blue poison." Jerk. Yank limbs. Try to break free.

"This is not a good situation, I'm afraid. Given your state, I'm not completely sure you can comprehend the things I'm saying to you. But, I have to try."

Doctor hesitates. Blows breath. Studies hands.

"We need to give you something called contrast material. It's another injection. It won't hurt, and it's not a sedative. A few seconds of patience, and this will all be over with. One injection, then a quick scan."

'Don't you worry. This will all be over soon. You won't remember a thing. Well, not enough to matter, Big Boy.'

Her voice. In my head. Her words. Not mine.

Panic rises. Body shakes. Fight restraints. Raise head. Slam on gurney. Again. Again. Again.

Doctor reaches out. Holds skull still. Hand under. Can't move.

"No, James!" he commands. "This is our last chance. You have to stop. I can't help you if you don't stop thrashing."

Turn head to side. Lash out. Target Doctor.

Bite. Bite hard. Teeth in arm. Gnashing. Buried deep.

Doctor cries out. Rips mouth away. Jumps back. Falls against big window.

Iron. Hot iron. On tongue. On chin. On neck.

"Pretty rabbit! Late! Late!" Throat burns. Stomach sick. Won't listen. Make him listen. Louder. "Stop! No! Stop! Down the hatch. Follow!"

Doctor knocks on glass. Polly runs. Leaves little room. Lifts Doctor's arm. Holds up. Inspects,

"Fuck," she hisses.

Grabs walkie. Radio static. Chirp.

"We need a nurse or a doctor in radiology, stat! Doctor Barrows is injured."

"I'm fine!" Doctor shouts. Takes breath. Clutches forearm. Grunts through teeth. "It's just a bite. Nothing more. See?" Shows Polly. "The wound isn't deep."

"Doctor, are you looking at the same thing I am? I see bone! Regardless, this man could have rabies or any number of diseases for all we know. I'm not taking any chances."

"No — Polly..." Doctor tries.

Andrew bursts in. Door bangs wall. Face purple. Enraged.

"What happened?" he demands. Rushes to Doctor.

"The patient attacked him." Polly furious. Moves Doctor behind wall. Behind glass. Can't see him. There, but gone.

Gone. All gone.

"Nononononono." Word keeps coming. Flowing like river. Salt in wound. "Blue poison," I cry. "Down the hatch."

More people. Andrew guides into other room. Join Doctor. Speak to Polly.

Same nurse comes. Stays back. Far away. Away.

Away from me.

Another doctor. Older. Rough. Hair gray and black. Forces my Doctor out of hiding.

Looks at Doctor's arm. Face blank. Thinking. Eyes flick. Studying. Barrows — me — Polly — Andrew — me again.

"Sedate him," Polly demands. "That man is a safety risk to everyone in this room. I want him sedated now."

"No." Doctor's voice firm. "Do not sedate that patient. It will not go well for anyone. I need to speak with him first. I can get through to him. I was getting through to him. I just need more time."

"What you need is to let us put him to sleep. This wound requires stitches." Andrew stern. "The restraints were not enough. What you're doing isn't working, Doctor Barrows."

"This is absurd." Doctor ignores. Tries to step toward me.

Andrew blocks him. Shakes head. Sits him down in other room.

Can't see him. Gone again.

"Whoever that patient is, he took a chunk of your forearm with his bite. The wound has not severed any arteries, but it's deep. There's damage to the skin and muscle. You're lucky he missed the tendon."

"I'm fine," Doctor insists.

"Sedate him, or I'll escort everyone out of this lab." Polly firm.

"It's the right choice," Andrew says.

"I agree," New Doctor adds.

My Doctor says nothing.

Silence. Heavy silence.

Deciding my fate.

"Haloperidol." New Doctor takes charge.

Quick movements. Nurse has needle. Vial. Draws fluid. Flicks tip. Drip. Drip. Drip.

Andrew takes needle. New Doctor comes. My Doctor stands. Leans on wall. Polly keeps him back. Watches me. Eyes sad.

"Please!" I call. "No! Please, no! Nonononono! Follow. Pretty rabbit. Follow. The hatch… the hatch is open. Follow!"

Restraints hold.

Needle nears.

Screaming. Hear my voice. Begging. Sobbing.

Slam head. Kick. Struggle. Strain. Jerk.

Andrew moves behind gurney. Hands on my temples. Firm. Strong.

No more fighting.

Pinch.

Arm numbs. World darkens.

"Blue poison. Drink me... Drink... Down... the..."

CHAPTER 12

NOW

"HE'S HEAVILY SEDATED." NOT DOCTOR. SOMEONE ELSE.

Man from room. Other doctor. New Doctor. Not mine. Assertive. Bored.

"It's unlikely he will wake for several hours."

"You shouldn't have done this," my Doctor answers. Voice angry. "I could have calmed him. I've done it before. We were building a relationship, and now, he'll likely believe I violated his trust."

Eyes won't open. Can't move. No restraints. Wrists free. Ankles free. Arms still heavy. Legs still heavy. Body numb. Hollow.

"What trust?" New Doctor asks. "You cannot establish trust with someone who doesn't have any idea who they are interacting with or what's going on around them. Honestly, Doctor Barrows. You're out of touch."

"Out of touch?" Doctor furious. "What's happening around here? Am I the only one who gives a damn about the standard of care we provide to our most vulnerable patients?" Loud footsteps. Pacing. Close by. "You're the one who is out of touch. We took an oath!"

"An oath to do no harm. That's exactly what I'm doing. I have stopped this man from injuring himself and others." Voice hard. New Doctor annoyed. "And, until I say otherwise, he will be heavily medicated. This facility cannot take the risk of letting your John Doe run wild."

"What you've done is deny this patient his freedom of choice. We owe him the truth. We owe him compassion and the right to be informed. We owe him an opportunity to make decisions related to his health."

"For fuck's sake, Greg!" Other doctor says. "If ever there was a time to declare someone incompetent, it's now. He doesn't even know his own goddamn name. How can we involve him, huh?"

Pacing stops. "We can attempt to speak with him rationally. We can make him feel like a human being. We can explain our reasoning before we do things and give him an opportunity to respond. While James may not fully understand what we say to him, we should say it nonetheless. We should give him the time and consideration he deserves!" Doctor's voice rough. Strained.

New Doctor scoffs. "You're wasting your time."

"It's my time to waste. I'll do with it as I please."

"You will not," New Doctor commands. "There are other patients on your caseload that you may actually be able to help. I am your superior, and I won't have you neglecting their care so you can fixate on a lost cause."

"Then, take them out of my care!" Doctor roars. Too loud. Ears throb. Quieter next. "I will not abandon James. He's not a lost cause. He's simply lost."

"His name is not James. You have no idea who this man is or what happened to him."

"I intend to find out."

Silence stretches. Tense.

Sleep calls.

New Doctor says, "I see. He's a puzzle, is that it? Something to prove yourself with? It won't matter, Doctor Barrows. Your status at this institution is rapidly dwindling. After what happened with the Thomas girl, I find it nigh impossible for you to recover your reputation anytime soon."

"He's not a fucking puzzle! He's a human being! Your lack of empathy is frankly disgusting. Don't make me call the board."

"Call them," New Doctor challenges. "I'd like to speak with them. They need to know how much you've fallen. Maybe this time, they'll send you on your way. How about that?"

"Leave," Doctor orders. "Now."

More silence. New sound. Heavy thud. Close to me. Papers flutter.

"If you want to destroy yourself, so be it." Steps toward door. "But, you should look at the scans first. Don't say I didn't warn you. You're as mad as he is if you refuse let this one go."

More steps.

"Haven't you heard? We're all mad here!" Doctor yells. "All of us. Patients. Staff. None of us can escape the trauma of this institution. Even you!"

No response.

Click. Door opens.

Whoosh. Door shuts.

Everything still.

Papers shuffle.

"What the fuck?" Doctor asks. No one answers. Mutters under breath. "That's impossible."

Bed sinks. Doctor sits. Mumbles quietly. More papers. More fluttering.

"I've never seen this much brain swelling in a conscious patient. How?"

Doctor inhales. Breath sharp. Papers stop.

"That's..." Doctor hesitates. "The... the pituitary is gone? Completely gone..."

Heavy breathing. Another thud. Doctor shifts. Leans over me. Touches forehand. Hand warm. Soft. Moves hair. Searches.

"But, there's no sign of surgery. The only injuries I can see are remnants of the suspected assault or self-inflicted. A procedure of this nature would have left signs, even if it had been performed by a skilled surgeon."

Turns head. Checks back. Sides. Behind ears. Touches nose. Mouth.

"Oh, James…" Trails off. "I…"

More silence.

Then, click. Door opens.

Footsteps. Door shuts.

"Doctor Barrows, the police are here." Andrew's voice.

Doctor stands. Walks away. Sounds nervous. Worried. "What's happening?"

"A man who matches your patient's description has been reported missing. They've come to take his fingerprints to see if we've found him."

"Thank God," Doctor answers. Calmer. "Perhaps, it will be good news." Sighs. "We're overdue for some."

"So I've heard."

"Let's not keep them waiting."

Door clicks. Opens.

Footsteps. Closes.

Both gone.

Sleep takes hold.

CHAPTER 13
NOW

MACHINE BEEPS. SOMETHING DRIPS.

Sounds start quiet. Get louder. Strange rhythm. Behind head.

So tired. Groggy. Was asleep. Now, awake. Barely.

Confused. Floating. Unattached. Bodiless. Weightless.

Doesn't last.

Settle slowly. Sink down. Discover flesh. Find my fingers. Wiggle toes. Move head.

Bed under me. Pillow. Mattress.

Body is cold. Too exposed. Bare skin. Thin gown. No blanket.

Restraints back. Not all. Less. Squeeze wrists. Bite ankles. None on chest. None on legs.

Too tight. Strapped down. Arms won't lift. Legs can't stretch.

Still trapped.

Monitor on finger. IV in elbow.

Something's different. Thinking simpler. Thoughts clearer. Dull, but there. Less scrambled. Easier to connect.

Blink slowly. Squint.

Lights too bright. Still buzzing. Never off.

Eyes won't focus. Room spins.

But… no wasps. No stinging. No maggots under skin. Bugs gone.

Sigh in relief. Less pain. No itching.

Deep breath. Difficult. Hurts too much.

Chest aches. Stiff. Sore.

Muscles weak. Quiver. Doesn't matter. Can't use anyway.

"Help…" My voice. Rough. Cracks. Try again. "H— help…"

Plea echoes. Bounces off walls. No one answers. No one listening. No one in room. It's empty.

Thirsty. Need to drink.

Drink…

Broken memory. Glass. Blue liquid. Sugar.

"Blue poison." Whisper faint. Throat too dry. Raspy. "Drink me. Down the hatch."

Hazy visions.

Not here. Somewhere else. Dark place. Flashing lights. People… people everywhere. Music. So loud. Thumping. Floor shaking.

Move away. Much quieter. Less people. Steel door.

Outside.

She's there.

"Follow…" I mumble. Lips stick together. Hard to understand. "Pretty rabbit."

Stale smoke. Dirty brick. Night sky. No stars. Clouds. Dumpsters. Garbage bags.

She turns. Watches me. Licks lips. Laughs. Blows white curls. Waits.

"Waiting. Pretty rabbit. Waiting."

Close eyes. Turn head. Nowhere to hide. No shield.

Tears gather. Run down cheeks. Stifle groan.

"Late."

Want to run. Change it. Make it stop. Get away. Forget her. Disappear.

"Too late."

Can't fight. Vision stays. Fragmented. Only splinters, but clear.

"Pretty rabbit. Waiting," I say. "Waiting for me."

Sparks on asphalt. Cigarette under shoe. Grinds. Takes my hand.

Fades to black. Memory gone. There, but not there.

Noise from hall. Outside door. Muffled voices. Several.

Can't hear. Too far away. Beeping and dripping too loud. Words too jumbled.

Try to back away. Remember restraints. Stuck. No cover.

Whimper. Defeated.

Door opens. Doctor comes. Not alone this time. Andrew follows. Close behind. Then, New Doctor. Nurse, too. Same one.

Too many. Too many people. Panic rising.

Cower. Shrink.

"If you insist on observing my treatment despite my vehement protests, you'll at least need to stay out of my way," Doctor orders.

Andrew listens. Leans against wall. Nurse joins him. New Doctor opens mouth. Wants to argue.

"This room is small enough as it is," Doctor adds. "My patient and I need space. You'll only make things worse by crowding him. He doesn't know you. We've built rapport. You haven't."

Doctor hates him. Despises.

Me too.

"Very well," New Doctor says. "I'll watch from here."

Door closes. New Doctor blocks it. Grins.

Doctor clenches jaw. Hands in pockets. Can see bunched fists. Comes closer to bed.

"It's great to see you awake." Sits on cot. Smiles. Kind. Patient. "You've been asleep for several hours, I'm afraid. However, I am happy to know that you've finally gotten some rest. Does it help? Are you feeling better?"

Anger. Surprises me. Hot in my veins. Doctor hurt me. Used restraints. Needles. Drugs.

"Get away!" I yell. Tug on bonds.

Doctor's face sinks. Disappointed.

Don't care.

"I am sorry about the restraints. Neither sedating you nor confining you to your bed was my decision. Given the episodes you've had, my colleagues have grown wary. You see, past experience has tainted them, I'm afraid. They believe you're dangerous."

Dangerous? Not dangerous. Terrified.

"I've attempted to explain that this is not the case. You and I were doing quite alright on our own, excluding the incident in radiology." Doctor turns head to crowd. "Prior, you had shown no indication of wishing to cause unprovoked harm, and I still do not believe you would have done so if we had not put you in a stressful situation, which I maintain is a direct result of interference in my patient's treatment," he spits.

New Doctor scoffs. Nurse cringes. Andrew blank.

"You're not dangerous. We both know better. What you are is injured, traumatized, and scared. And, who wouldn't be? They don't understand. I'm sorry about that, too."

Stop tugging. Arms and legs limp. Body still. Take shallow breaths.

"That's it," Doctor says. "Remember where you are. Remember me. I know you can do it. You've done it before. You have nothing to fear from me. Not now, not ever. Do you understand?"

Do I? I am afraid. *Afraid of Doctor?*

No. Afraid of them.

"Can we start with a deep breath? That always helps me. Like this." Doctor breathes. Shoulders rise. Sink back down. Exhales. Parted lips.

Try. Chest still aches. Lungs resist. First one shallow. Try again. In. Out. Blow. Another breath.

"Good. Control your fear," Doctor praises. "Show my colleagues that you are no threat to me or to them. In time, they may allow me to remove your bindings if you can do so. Would you like that to happen?"

Blow out breath. Nod head.

"Thank you for sharing your feelings with me. I can see your attempts, and I value them. It must be difficult in your situation. I may not know what, but I recognize that you've been through things I likely can't even begin to fathom."

Touch of calm. Heart still races. Breath still hitches. But, feeling better.

"Is it helping?" Doctor tilts head.

"Y… yes." Lips tremble.

New Doctor frowns.

"Good. I can't bear the thought of you being in distress. I would like for you to be more comfortable. It will take some time, but we'll get there. I am a healer. We all are. We want to help you heal."

Healers? Maybe Doctor. Not them. Not with needles. Not with restraints. Not with choking. Drugs.

Doctor cares. Others don't. They're different.

"I have some news that I'd like to share with you. Would you like to hear it?"

Hesitate. Think. Look at crowd.

Andrew shifts. Expressions all curious. Watchful. No one angry.

Nod head.

"I will warn you, not all of what I have to say will be positive. Still, it is important."

Doctor squeezes hand.

"Though what happened in radiology was unfortunate, something good came of it. We were able to give you a CT scan, primarily focused on your brain." Doctor pauses. Considers words. "I won't lie to you. Never. You deserve to understand your situation, at least as much as you can."

Doctor shifts on bed. Lips thin. Eyes sad.

"What we found on your scan is concerning. You've had significant brain trauma. That much, we expected. There was unprecedented swelling. If we hadn't intervened, the results could have been deadly."

Deadly? Death. *Death would be kinder.* Thought so before. Hasn't changed now.

"I've administered a medication that should help. Steroids. A second scan indicates they are working, though if they should stop doing so, we may need to implement a shunt. We can discuss this if the need arises.

Swelling? Head throbs.

"But, what's most worrisome is something else entirely. Which brings me to an important question. I know you have difficulty remembering, but I'm forced to ask regardless. This is too important to leave to chance. If you have any information for us, it must come to light. So, I need you to try very hard. Can you do that?"

Swallow. Nod head.

Doctor begins again. "Thank you. Focus. Stay with me." Locks eyes on mine. " Have you undergone any recent surgeries, particularly having to do with your brain or pituitary gland?"

"S… sur… surgeries?" I ask.

Scalpels. Knives. Cuts. Stitches.

"Yes. Have you had any surgeries? Was your pituitary removed recently?"

Think. Think hard. Search thoughts. Dig for memory.

Remember hearing Doctor. Him studying skull.

But, surgeries?

Nothing. Blank.

Confused. Shake head.

Doctor sighs. Sad. "Then, we have another mystery, I'm afraid. I'll admit, I rather expected you either would not know or would not have had such a surgery, but it was worth a try. I promise you, I will continue searching for answers."

New Doctor snickers. My Doctor glares. Andrew straightens.

"This is unfortunate," Doctor replies. "Yet, I appreciate your answer, regardless. Your input is valuable. I see that you're trying. So am I."

Not valuable. Not worthy. Gave nothing. Remember nothing.

Frustration. Fear. Despair.

Shut eyes.

Want to give up.

"It's not all bad news, though." Smile returns to Doctor's face. "It seems your mental clarity has improved. The medication has brought about positive changes. Would you agree?"

Don't answer.

"You're much more calm, and I can see thoughts processing differently in your mind. That's wonderful. If we can make things easier on you, we may find answers sooner. In fact, we've found one already."

Eyes snap open. Breath hitches.

"You may have noticed I have not been referring to you as 'James' during our conversation. Did you?"

No. Shake head. More confused. Curious.

"That's quite alright. Well, there's a reason for this, I can assure you. While you were asleep, we made contact with law enforcement." Joy in Doctor's smile. "Someone matching your description has been reported missing. Police officers took your fingerprints and found a match."

Stunned silence.

"We know your name."

Name. *My name?* My name. Not James. Real. Mine.

"It's a pleasure to re-introduce myself to you today," Doctor says. "I'm Doctor Gregory Barrows, and you, my friend, are Riley Sylers."

CHAPTER 14

THEN

Braxton (10:01 am): Hey man! What a night!

Braxton (10:01 am): Sorry to leave u @ the club. Didn't wanna cramp ur style.

Braxton (10:01 am): Dynah was a shit lay btw. Spent half the night puking.

Braxton (10:02 am): Did u get into the bartender's pants?

Braxton (10:02 am): Or somebody's?

Missed Call

Braxton (11:15 am): U did didn't u? Sneaky bastard. Celeste is gonna b so damn jealous. Tell me u got pictures. U need 2 show off!

Braxton (11:16 am): Man fuck her. Good 4 u. U deserve a break.

Braxton (11:16 am): Riley! Come on! Don't leave me hanging dickwad!

Braxton (11:17 am): ???

Missed Call

Braxton (2:09 pm): Fuck! Musta been a helluva night. R u awake yet?

Missed Call

Braxton (2:52 pm): Whatever. Sleep it off. Just lemme know ur alive when u get this k?

Missed Call
Missed Call

Braxton (8:38 pm): Dude where r u?

Missed Call
Missed Call
Missed Call

Braxton (11:22 pm): Ur freakin me out. Answer me or I'm coming over.

Missed Call
Missed Call

Braxton (11:30 pm): I'm not kidding man. I got the cops on speed dial. I'm getting in the car.

Braxton (11:53 pm): I'm @ ur place. Lemme in.

Missed Call
Missed Call

Braxton (12:04 am): K fine. Ur car's not here. Maybe ur not home. I'm going back 2 the club.

Braxton (12:41 am): Fuck dude! Y is ur car still in the structure? R u @ the bar? If u went without me I'm kicking ur ass.

Missed Call

Braxton (01:16 am): K... so ur not here...

Braxton (01:29 am): Nobody @ the club knows who u went home with. I'm seriously freaked. Where the fuck r u? Come on Riley. Call me back.

Missed Call
Missed Call

Braxton (2:08 am): I'm calling the cops.

CHAPTER 15

THEN

MY GLASS IS EMPTY.

I hadn't meant to, but as soon as Allison had left, I'd swallowed most of the cocktail in an ill-fated attempt to soothe my burnt tongue. My dumb ass forgot that alcohol stings. It had only made it worse. Once the pain finally subsided, the rest of the drink followed the greasy mushrooms down the hatch. Now, the remaining few drops of blue liquid cling to the sides of my cup, slowly sliding to the bottom.

There's not even a sip left.

Part of me knows this is far too much liquor. If nothing else, I should drink some water. If I don't, I'll be sick as a dog in the morning. I should probably find some ibuprofen, too. But, I really couldn't care less.

See, that's a problem for *future* Riley.

Present Riley is more concerned with the empty appetizer basket.

I'm hungry. Insatiably so. Hungrier than I've been in a long time.

Sure, Braxton and I had pizza for dinner, but that was hours ago, and the DoorMouse is notorious for skimping on toppings. That's why they're the cheapest pizzeria around. Their food is sufficient when I have no plans to leave the house, but that's not how tonight played out.

I was ready to eat again by the time we'd left my apartment. Adding alcohol didn't help. Plus, those mushrooms? Now, they were a delicious snack.

Then again, everything Allison has brought me tonight has been incredible.

She's incredible. A fucking goddess. A delicious snack in her own right. If only my dream girl would come back...

Am I hungry for food or am I hungry for her? The first option would be easier, yet I've got a nagging suspicion it's the second that has my mouth watering. Braxton may have set the challenge, but reluctant as I may be to admit it, I'm starting to think she's exactly the right cure for my depression.

I want her. The more I think about her, the more I'm sure of it.

But, Allison's been gone for a while. Or, it feels like she has? It's getting harder to keep my thoughts straight. Time is a lot less important now that I'm drowning in intoxicated bliss.

Well, it would be bliss if the club would stop moving. The bar sways like a ship in a fierce storm, rocking this way and that. I know it isn't real, just a result of the alcohol, yet I can't help but hold fast to the edge of the sticky top.

The problem is my body is much lighter than it was when I sat down. Except for my head. My arms and legs are made of cork, moving a little too easily, but my head feels like an anchor, the only thing keeping me from drifting away.

Damn, when did I become a pirate? A quiet chuckle escapes me. This isn't the open ocean. I'm not sailing in a sea of self-pity. I mean, I was when I got here, but I'm done wailing over Celeste. She made her choice. Screw her and her picture-perfect life. I don't want that.

Cannon fire in the form of booming bass fires from the speakers. My chest pounds and my stomach swirls. Music vibrates through my bones. The air reeks of sweat and sex.

That's not helping.

It's too loud, and I'm getting bored. No, that's not it. Not bored. Lonely. Exhausted. I'm sinking. It's getting late, and I'm fading fast. I'm too tired to sit here much longer without passing out.

I need to find Allison. Convince her I'm not just some moron who swaggered up to her bar with an overinflated sense of self-importance. Show her I'm not like the rest, that I'm actually worth going home with.

It's gotta be after midnight by now. Probably closer to one, I'd guess. The club will be closing soon. I might as well give it all I've got.

She said she likes weak men. Time to see if that's true. If it applies to me.

But, where the hell has my sexy little rabbit scurried off to?

Pushing myself to my feet, I abandon the bar stool. The full rush of alcohol slams into me when I manage to stand. Like that, I'm reduced to a college freshman, left unattended at his first frat party. Allison's drinks are more powerful than any Jungle Juice. The world flips, then rights itself, then flips back.

It's disorienting and rather nauseating, but I won't let it stop me.

Determined, I leave Braxton's fifty on the counter and add another twenty of my own for good measure. That should be enough. To be honest, I probably overpaid.

Unsteady, I weave through the throng. Depth perception be damned. The passage stretches and contracts with each step. Several dancers level angry glares at me as I accidentally shoulder-check them when I pass. I mumble apologies, hoping they can hear me over the techno beat, and make my way to the front of the club, following the same path my friend and his "date" had.

Cool air envelopes me as the door swings open into the night. Leaning against the steel frame for support, I survey the remarkably empty alley. All the lights are out. Still no crowd. No traffic passing by. More importantly, no Allison here, either.

Just Antonio, or whatever the hell his name really is. The bouncer is busy scrolling on his phone to pass the time. When he notices me, he looks up with a mildly interested expression.

"Your douchebag friend left with a regular over an hour ago," he says. "Figured you'd be gone by now, too. Don't entitled dicks travel in packs?"

"Usually," I answer, unashamed. "He ditched me. Found a date."

"Some date. Dynah was trashed. Guess he's not one for chivalry." Disgust tinges the man's words.

I can't disagree, so I nod. That's a mistake. My eyes lose focus, and bile rises in my throat. I manage to keep it down, but only barely.

"Fuck man, so are you. Tell me you didn't drive." Antonio tenses.

"Ugh, I drove," I admit. My hand flies to my forehead as though it could halt the vertigo. "Parked in the structure."

The bouncer shakes his head. "You better go back to the bar and have them call you a cab. I'd hate to have to take your keys."

"I'm not leaving yet." Raising my fist, I grind it into my eyes next. It does nothing to steady the planet. "I'm looking for someone."

"There ain't no one out here but me, and I can't have you standing in the doorway all night. In or out. It's a liability," Antonio demands.

"So, you haven't seen her? Allison? She said she was going for a smoke."

Even drunk, it's impossible not to notice the shift in the bouncer's posture. His frame goes rigid at the mention of the bartender's name.

"Fucking idiots. One after another," he grumbles. He gazes behind me into the club, then snaps his attention back to the alley. "Give up while you're ahead. Just admit you struck out and go home. She's not the one for you."

"I'm not like Braxton. I've got a chance." Honestly, I'm not sure that's true, but whatever. "Where's she go to smoke?" I ask.

Antonio hesitates. He looks me over consideringly. His mouth turns down, and his expression shifts to something akin to sad resignation.

"Out back." He points farther down the alley to where the brick wall splits. A chain link gate creaks on its hinges, swaying slightly. "But, you should know something. Around here, we call Allison the Queen of Hearts. She's always got someone following her. Most of them never come back. She's a maneater, that one."

"I could do with someone like that."

"Suit yourself." He gives up his efforts to dissuade me. "Don't say I didn't warn ya."

Antonio grabs me by the shoulder and shoves me out of the club. The steel door slams behind me with a loud "smack," cutting off all sound from inside. I'm at the swinging gate before I even register that my feet have carried me down the alley.

"You're not Antonio, are you?" I call back to the bouncer, pausing.

"Hell no. Not even close." He grimaces.

"What's your real name, then?" I ask.

"Chester," he says with disinterest. "Not that it matters. I'll never see your stupid face again."

I was right. His name wasn't Antonio after all.

With that, I leave him behind.

CHAPTER 16

THEN

IN THE DARK, EVERYTHING IS BLURRY AROUND THE EDGES. IT'S DIFFICULT TO see the obstacles in my path. Twice, I trip over deep cracks in the alley's asphalt before emerging from the other side. A second door to the club has been propped open. Flashing lights stain the ground and illuminate Allison's form. Music, muted by distance from the dance floor, courses through the air.

Casually, she leans against the side of an overflowing dumpster, cigarette in hand. The white smoke curling from her fingers seems almost to be tinted with blue as it drifts toward the night sky.

Allison doesn't notice me at first, but rather keeps her eyes glued to the brick wall, captivated by something I can't discern from this far away. Narrowly avoiding a head-on collision with the emergency exit sign jutting from the side of the building, I make my way over to where she stands.

A small caterpillar, no bigger than the first length of my pinky, inches its way across the rough mortar. Allison blows a puff of smoke in its direction. The insect wriggles, then disappears behind the garbage bin.

"Thought you might have ditched me," I say, announcing my presence. She doesn't jump. My arrival must not have come as a surprise.

Wearing a sarcastic grin, Allison turns to face me. "What, and miss all of your antics? Not a chance." She stubs out her cigarette and tosses it into the dumpster. "I've only been out here for ten minutes."

"Felt like longer," I admit. "Must be the drinks."

"Must be." Straightening up, Allison stretches, revealing the soft curve of her stomach and that pocket watch tattoo trailing along her squeezable hip again. "I did mix you up something special. Gave it my... everything." She licks her lips. "Is it working?"

Confusion settles over my features. "Working how?"

"Lowering your inhibitions. Giving you false courage. You know, the usual alcoholic machismo but with a tug toward adventure thrown in."

"Absolutely," I answer. "I'm lighter than air and ready to take a shot at the sexy bartender if that's what you mean."

Allison laughs, a real laugh this time, not some half-hearted scoff. The sound is incredibly appealing, like tinkling bells on the wind. "Is that so?"

"Mmm," I groan, taking several steps in her direction. She doesn't back away. That's a good sign. "It is."

I hadn't realized how much shorter she is. Sitting on the stool leveled the playing field. Compared to my six feet, she's pint-sized, maybe five four? Her dainty white hair bow comes up to the center of my chest, and her shoulders align with my ribs.

God, I fucking love short women. The way they have to tip their heads back to look at me. How tight and compact their frames are.

"Well, go ahead then," she suggests. "Take your shot. Watch it miss."

Allison's chest rises in challenge as I close the distance between us and press my palms to the dumpster at either side of her head, boxing her in. Her breaths are steady, but there's something in the way she stares at me that screams desire and mischief.

Those eyes, like molten metal. The perfect slope of her nose. The way her bangs settle against her eyebrows, showing just a hint of the creamy skin underneath.

She's irresistible.

I'm losing control over myself simply by being in her presence. Things have changed since I arrived at The Rabbit Hole with Braxton. *I've* changed. Desire courses through me, growing stronger by the minute.

She knew exactly what she was doing with those drinks.

Lowering my head to hers, I inhale the scent of her perfume. It smells like sugar and vanilla, like a frosted cookie or a cupcake. A dessert that will forever leave me craving more. I bet her lips will taste just as sweet.

But, does she want me to kiss her? Will she let me?

Bending until the top of my nose connects with the curve of her neck, I drag it up, feeling the softness of her skin, only stopping when my mouth is level with her ear. "You said you like us weak," I whisper. "What did you mean?"

Allison chuckles. For a moment, she hesitates, contemplating her answer.

"Easily manipulated," she replies. "I find pleasure in watching you pine after something you can't have or tugging you along on a leash if you've got a chance. See, I'm not like other women. I don't do love or relationships. Men are simply things to be played with. I use them, I take what I want, and move on."

I shift so that my mouth hovers only inches from hers. Cherry lipstick, faintly smudged by her cigarette, coats her plump lips. They part slightly, sucking in a shallow breath.

"Play with me tonight," I suggest. "Use me for whatever you'd like and toss me aside. I don't care."

She studies me, considering. The alley tilts under my feet, rocked by another wave of vertigo, but I manage to stay standing.

Allison's eyes drift to a silver watch on her wrist. "It's late," she says.

"It is," I agree. "Isn't it time we went to bed?"

She sighs and closes her eyes, shaking her head. "I never even asked your name."

"Riley." My lips brush against hers, and goosebumps pop up all over my skin.

Allison accepts the touch, leaning into my body and deepening the kiss. My hands find the swell of her hips as her tongue dances in an electric rhythm with mine. Tantalizing. Teasing. Caressing. She nips at my lower lip.

I could spend eternity like this.

When we break free, she says, "You don't want to go home with me, Riley. You seem like a nice guy. You don't understand. I'll break you."

My answer is simple. "Break me, then."

"A night with me will change your life, moron." There's warning in her tone.

"That's the plan," I admit. In the absence of her lips, my own begin to tingle, just as they had from the drinks.

Allison leans her head back against the dumpster and grimaces. "The plan. They always have a plan." Her words aren't meant for me. They're more like grumbles to the universe at large. "They never listen."

"Please, Allison." I close my eyes and lower my forehead to hers. "Shatter me into a million pieces. I want this. I need you."

Allison's golden eyes bore into mine. She groans. Pressing her hands into my chest, she shoves me away. "Remember you said that," she commands.

Stumbling backward, I catch myself with one arm against the club's exterior. "I couldn't possibly forget."

"We'll see about that." Allison pushes up onto her tiptoes and offers me the sweetest kiss, as faint as the flutter of a butterfly's wings. "We have a deal then. One night with me, doing whatever I please, and I send you packing by dawn. Got it?"

"Deal," I agree. Desperate to feel her touch again, I reach for her.

She swats my hand away and rips the scrunchie from her hair, securing it around her wrist. "I'm off in twenty minutes. Stay here, Riley. I'll take you to my place. But I promise you, I won't hold back."

She doesn't wait for me to answer, simply abandons me in the alley, shutting the door behind her and disappearing.

A faint tinge of iron dances on my tongue. The minutes tick by, and the colors of the world swirl together.

Twenty minutes...

Time no longer holds meaning. In the blink of an eye, Allison once more emerges from The Rabbit Hole's rear exit. A thin white jacket covers her torso. A small black purse dangles from her shoulder. In one of her hands, a white rabbit's foot keychain dangles.

"Let's go, then," she insists.

Clutching my arm, she drags me back down the alley toward the main entrance. She's quick on her feet, much more adept than I am. We pass through the gate, and she slams it shut behind us.

Chester no longer stands guard by the door. A stream of patrons exit. The once vacant street fills with slurred voices and drunk customers.

The Rabbit Hole must be closed. *It really is late.*

Allison vigilantly scans our surroundings as we pass one street, then the next, and the next. Her footfalls are light, and I stumble along behind her almost blindly, lost to the world except for her guidance.

It doesn't take long before we stop in front of an apartment building, one that's seen better days. The lower homes have bars over their windows. None of them are open to the evening breeze. Inside, the lights are off or blocked by heavy blinds and curtains. Again, the streetlights above us flicker.

Unlike my building, this one is unlocked, apparently open to all who seek to enter. Allison jerks the door open and ushers me inside, then tugs me up several flights of stairs. The air is stale and reeks of weed, among other things.

We reach the fifth-floor landing — *I think it's the fifth-floor?* I've lost track. A shadowy hallway looms ahead of us, lit only by faint yellow light from old fixtures. The space is narrow, lined with residences on either side. We pass them by, one after another, until Allison abruptly halts, sticks a key into a battered knob, and turns to face me.

Her white rabbit's foot keychain dangles from the lock, and her hand rests lightly atop the scuffed steel. I have enough presence of mind to notice the paint is flaking off the door, but not much else. I'm too fixated on the woman before me to care.

A mass of thick, blonde hair falls to just below her shoulders. The white bow pinning back the top section remains in place. It's probably not intentional, but it makes her look so innocent. It gives off a school-girl vibe, and I can't say I'd want it any other way.

A dark look flashes across her features as she watches me sway on my feet. I can't tell if she's annoyed, concerned, or curious.

"This is your last chance, Riley. I hate to say it, but I kind of like you. You're cute, in an awkward sort of way." The key turns in the lock with a clink. "You don't have to do this. I can call you a cab. You can go home."

"Fuck no," I answer without hesitation. "There's nothing for me there. I want you. I'd follow my white rabbit anywhere."

Allison blinks, and in a trick of the light, again her golden eyes gleam like garnets. This time, they don't fade back to that luscious gild. She cocks her head to the side and bites her bottom lip, pushing open the apartment door. It creaks on its hinges, revealing the obsidian black-ness within.

"Alright," she says, disappearing inside. "A deal's a deal. Down the rabbit hole, then."

I chuckle at her callback to the club's name, but she shushes me.

"Come on. It's getting late. Don't wake my sisters."

Allison doesn't bother to turn on the lights. She doesn't need them to navigate her home. Instead, she reaches for my hand. The soft fur of the keychain brushes against my exposed wrist as she tugs me deeper and deeper, away from the rest of the world.

The apartment is bigger than it seemed from the hall. Like a child, she tows me past several rooms, all shut up tightly. Vaguely, I'm aware that we should have reached the end, but it doesn't matter.

Impossible stairs appear to our left, and I follow her up, up, up, and up. By the time we reach the top, I'm out of breath.

There's only one room up here. Hers. This door is open, and purple and blue neon lights illuminate the interior.

Allison stops, giving me a decent view of what awaits.

The space is huge. A plush four-poster bed rests in the center of the floor. A thick, white duvet, perfectly smoothed, is spread across the top. Someone, probably her, has scattered blue rose petals across the surface of the blanket. Several pillows rest against the headboard. A trunk sits by the footboard, and two solid nightstands adjoin each side of the bed's frame.

Stepping through the threshold, she pulls me along with her. Once I'm completely inside, she closes the door softly behind us, and turns the lock, sealing us in.

There's much more in this room than I saw from the hall. My eyes widen as I take in the many treasures that were hidden just out of sight.

I've never seen these things in person before, only in the porn Braxton insists on sending me. I know what they're for, but as for how to use them... well, that's another issue.

A St. Andrew's Cross stands in the corner, an impeccable 'X,' wood stained red and polished to a shimmer. Black leather cuffs dangle from each point. A table of toys stands next to it, all neatly arranged.

Across from the toy table, a sex swing hangs from the ceiling by a heavy bolt. This is adjacent to the floor to ceiling window that looks out over the street, towering above several surrounding buildings. Nestled in front of the thick glass sits a bench, covered in silky fabric and blue velvet. More cuffs hang from both ends. Even more toys are displayed nearby on a wall. There are no curtains. The entire city is visible.

My mouth falls open in awe. Turning back to Allison, I manage to grit out, "What is this place?"

A flirtatious smile adorns her face. She uses two fingers to shut my mouth before answering. "Welcome to Wonderland, Riley. I'm so glad you came to visit."

CHAPTER 17

NOW

"DOES THAT NAME SOUND FAMILIAR TO YOU?" DOCTOR ASKS. EYES WATCH me with interest. Hopeful. Eager. "Do you recall the name Riley Sylers?"

Riley... Riley Sylers?

Not familiar.

Still, a name. Real one. Not like "James." Temporary. Fake.

But, my name? *Is it?* Maybe... Could be.

Has to be there. Some trace. Some clue. Hidden inside. Locked away from me. Held prisoner.

Prisoner. Word makes me shiver. That feels familiar. Eyes travel to cuffs on wrists. Ankles.

No memory of Riley. Of who I was. Anyone other than this.

Trapped. Afraid. Lost and empty.

I am no one. Nobody important. Broken man. Blank canvas.

So, my name?

Doctor says Riley. Took fingerprints. Spoke to police. Has proof.

Still, tricky problem. Trust Doctor? Hard question to answer. Thought so, but...

Trust him *sometimes*. Not with needles. Not with restraints. Betrayed me before. Might do it again.

But, with this?

Always wants to help. To fix me. Find out what happened. At least, he claims.

Doesn't lie. Give him that. Defends me against New Doctor. Stopped Andrew. Keeps coming back.

Yes, I decide. *Trust him now. Trust him with this.*

He must know. Must be certain. Have right name.

Riley Sylers.

Still not there, but accept.

"No," I answer. "Gone." Swallow. Watch Doctor's expression.

Doctor's face falls. Not defeated, but not happy. "I had hoped that knowing your name would bring about more recollection of your life and circumstances," Doctor admits. Picks at nails. Nervous habit.

Uncomfortable in bed. Try to adjust body. Cuffs hold in place. Shift only inches.

Cot creaks. Pillow drops to floor. Head thumps to mattress. Makes me wince.

"It's tricky, trying to uncover truths with such potent amnesia. Some-times, information is like a magical key that grants you access to all you have forgotten, or at least enough of it that things begin to come together more sensibly. However, sometimes information is just that — information."

Retrieves pillow. Puts under my head. Settles back into seat. Hands clasp in lap. Fingers twine together.

Something clicks into place. Unexpected. Jarring.

Key. Word has meaning. Lodges in brain. Causes me to react.

Hands seize. Release. Ball into fists. Spasm and grip edge of mattress.

Compelled by body. Not by mind.

"Key" is important. But, why? Reason?

What is key? Key shuts. Opens. Locks things. Unlocks things. Cars. Gates. Chests. Doors.

Doors…

Yes, doors. Guarded entrances. Locked up tight. Then, released.

Key reveals what's hidden. Empty rooms. Dark hallways. Impossible stairs.

Up, up, up… Climb higher. Follow pretty rabbit.

Follow where?

To secret places. Away from others. Help. Reality.

Follow to… Wonderland.

Limbs freeze. Incredibly cold. Chest aches. Breath falters. Stomach churns.

"Your predicament seems inclined to the latter option, I'm afraid. Only time can provide us with answers in such positions."

Not listening. Focusing. Focusing on new name.

Wonderland. A place? Somewhere good? Bad? Exciting? Terrifying? Everything in between?

"Please don't mistake my meaning," Doctor continues. "To clarify, Riley, It is simply information for now, not forever. And, information is useful. You may not know what has happened to you, but perhaps we can complete some of the puzzle for you while we wait for your mind to recover. As I've said, the steroid treatment we've administered is already reducing critical swelling. Given time and the marvels of modern medicine, who knows what we can accomplish together, you and I."

A place, but not a place. A room. Hidden. Secret.

Down the hall. Up the stairs. Step inside. Roses. Windows. Bed.

"In fact, we've already learned one crucial thing just by discovering your name, Riley. You have a friend, the man who reported you missing. We took the liberty of calling him and asking him to come here this evening. He's waiting just at the end of the hall for permission to enter."

She was there. Right there. Right beside me. *In Wonderland…*

"If you'd like, I can ask your friend to join us now. If not, he can be escorted out at your discretion."

Door closes behind us. Room dark. Spins. Strange lights. Trapped inside. Danger. In danger.

"What do you say, Riley?" Doctor waits. Watches. Listens.

Heart pounds. Try to calm. Try to breathe. Come back to Doctor. Escape vision. Run from memory.

But, her eyes… crimson.

They see me.

"Do you remember having a friend, Riley?" Doctor prompts. Touches hand. Commands me to look. Voice gentle. "This man's name is Braxton. By his account, the two of you were close. I believe seeing him may help you get your bearings."

Focus on Doctor. Focus on Doctor. Focus on Doctor.

Stay out of Wonderland.

"All I require is your consent for the visitation to allow him inside. A simple nod will do, or a shake of the head will suffice to deny permission."

Permission? For what? Listening now.

Oh, friend. Have a friend?

Friend means safety. Friend means memory? Friend means... friend means...

What does friend mean?

Braxton.

Key twists inside head. Lock opens. See a face. Dark hair. Crinkled eyes. Clean shaven.

His face? Braxton's face. My friend?

Need to know. See if the face matches. See if it belongs to Braxton. Test memory.

Nod head. Give permission.

Want it to match. Good distraction. Want to forget what I saw. Not ready. Too much fear.

Something else, too. Different feeling. What is it? Can't place it.

"Excellent," Doctor replies. Genuine smile. Rises from bed. "Allow me a moment to retrieve him." Moves to door. Touches Andrew's shoulder. "I believe we will be in need of a chair."

"Are you sure that's a good idea?" Andrew asks. Concerned. Pinched face.

"As good as any," Doctor states. "Braxton will require a place to sit while they get reacquainted. Seeing his friend like this may be a shock. He will likely not want to seat himself on the bed as I have."

Doctor opens door. Nurse dashes out. Doesn't look back. Thrilled to get away.

Other doctor hesitates. Stares. Eyes me with disdain. Follows Nurse. So does Andrew.

Doctor waits. Says one last thing.

"I know it's hard, but if you can, be patient with Braxton, Riley. From what I can tell, you mean a lot to him. It will be hard for him to see you this way. Do you understand?"

Patient. Hard. Friend...

Nod head.

Doctor turns. Steps out into hall. Shuts door behind him.

Footsteps disappear.

Alone again.

CHAPTER 18
THEN

"WONDERLA—" IS ALL I HAVE TIME TO SAY BEFORE ALLISON'S MOUTH crashes into mine with unexpected violence. Her soft, plump lips cut off my words, and her tongue coaxes me into willful submission, gliding artfully over my own. The question I'd been about to ask fades from my thoughts completely when she playfully bites my lower lip.

Caught off guard, I let out a groan of pain and anticipation. I want more of that. So much more. And, I want it *now*.

Allison buries her fingers in my hair, deepening the kiss. Heat surges to my groin as every muscle in my body coils. I haven't felt so alive in months. Her deliberate seduction awakens something feral in me. Inside my jeans, my dick answers her call, hardening until it strains against my zipper.

In a flash, she has the fabric of my shirt balled up in her fist. Somehow, she manages to guide me toward the awaiting bed without breaking contact. She's nimble on her feet, carefully avoiding the footboard, whereas I'm a stumbling mess. We collapse onto the mattress in a delicious tangle of arms and legs. The rose petals she'd so carefully strewn onto the bed fly into the air, scattering around us. Their silky touch as they flutter back onto the comforter makes me shiver.

Allison withdraws first, just long enough so the two of us can inhale a few quick breaths. For those seconds, her absence is palpable. My skin burns everywhere she's touched like it's raw, as though without her, part of it is missing.

"Take it off," she commands. Her capable fingers tug at the hem of my shirt, insistent. "Take it off, now."

In a rush, I let her guide the fabric up and over my head, then allow it to fall to the floor beside us. It lands quietly amid a pile of petals, sending up their sickly sweet scent.

Allison's eyes widen as they trail over my body, wandering from my face down to my shoulders, my chest, and my stomach. "Fuck, Riley... You were hiding all that?"

I linger for a moment, letting her see me for the first time.

An impish grin spreads across her swollen lips. Without hesitation, she reaches for my biceps and gives them a firm squeeze. Satisfied, she lets go and skims her nails across my pecs, then traces the indentations of my abs down to the waistband of my pants, making goosebumps erupt across my skin. Her expression simmers with hunger, a reaction that stokes my fire.

Bracing myself on my forearms, I lean back into her body, keeping the bulk of my weight off of her frame.

But, Allison isn't having that. Not for one minute. Catching me off guard, her strong arms draw me into a tight embrace. She trails eager nibbles along my shoulder as her palms find their way against the flat of my back. Her nails replace the soft touch of her palms, biting into me. Again, I grunt from a mixture of pleasure and pain.

"I'm going to devour you," she whispers. "Every inch. Just not yet."

"God," I grumble. My cock throbs with need. *What is this woman doing to me?* I'm putty in her hands. Wasn't that what she was supposed to be? Braxton's earlier words ring through my head. *My, how the tables have turned.*

Allison shoves me onto my knees and allows me to tug her shirt off, discarding it beside my own. Another groan tears free from my throat, this one verging on desperation. My heart stutters in my chest when I catch sight of what was waiting just beneath her top.

I was right. *Holy shit, was I fucking right.* She wasn't wearing a bra at the club, and now, the proof is here in front of me.

Allison settles back onto the pillows, and her ample breasts bounce. They look like heaven, soft as clouds. Her nipples, the perfect shade of pink, are hard enough to cut glass.

I've never been this aroused.

I'm overcome with the absolute need to worship her, to lower my head and bury it between her tits, to suck those perky little nubs into my mouth, languishing my tongue over the ridges until she's squirming beneath me.

Allison has other plans.

"Take off my pants," she orders, but I'm hypnotized by what I can already see of her body. She plants the sole of her foot against my chest and pushes, just enough to draw back my attention. "I said, take off my pants."

"Fuck, yes."

Allison doesn't move. She simply waits for me to follow instructions. Obediently, I do exactly that.

Keeping my eyes trained on her and not bothering to pop the button, I drag them down by the ankles, revealing the wicked curves of her hips. A delicate little white lace thong hides her pussy. My dick twitches at the mere sight of it, the pretty fabric covering her cunt like a specially chosen gift. It's the only present I've ever needed, one I'm especially excited to unwrap.

Eager to staunch the craving growing inside of me, I reach for my jeans, ready to abandon them right this second. My fingers are already working the button when Allison smacks my hand. My eyes snap to hers, confused and pleading.

"Down boy," she insists. Fire smolders in her gaze, laced with authority and mischief. "You're here to please me, Riley. Not yourself. I didn't give you permission to take off *your* pants."

I swallow hard. *Oh, how I want to please her.* My throat goes dry at the thought of all the delightfully naughty things I would love to do to this woman. Whatever she wants, no matter how depraved. She could ask me to run bare-ass naked through the streets, and I'd do it without a second thought. Her wish is my command.

I don't need to tell her any of this. Allison knows exactly what I'm thinking.

Biting her lower lip, she taunts me. "Get back over here," she commands. "I'm not through with that pretty mouth of yours yet."

Positioning myself directly above her, I let Allison haul my mouth back to hers, and we consume one another, luxuriating in each other's kisses until I barely remember who I am. It feels like this goes on for hours. All the while, the slightest touch of her bare skin against mine sends electric shocks through my core. Then, I abandon her lips and work my way down the dainty slope of her neck.

"Good boy." She sighs into my ear when I nip at the sensitive skin just above her breast. "Please me, Riley. Tonight, you're mine. There's no going back."

Immediately, her hands shove me lower, and I find myself face-to-face with her glorious chest. My palm closes over one of her supple tits, and *my* wish is finally granted. I claim one of her nipples, sucking it between my lips and letting my teeth graze over the bud. My tongue circles the raised peak, swirling and flicking. Allison shuts her eyes and leans back into the pillows, enjoying every second.

Keeping my mouth trained on her breast, I drag my hand down to the mesh covering her warm slit. Lightly, I slide my fingertip over the material, teasing her pussy. She angles her hips up toward me. The thin fabric, the only barrier separating her from my caress, is already soaked with her excitement.

Just as I'm about to slip the thong aside and dip my finger into her sweet core, Allison lets out the most delightful laugh.

"Riley," she breathes, turning her salacious eyes to mine.

"Yes?" I ask, unwilling to halt my assault on her chest for more than it takes to say the one word.

"I want more than just your fingers. I want your tongue. I want you to feast on my cunt like it's the last meal you'll ever have."

My eyes roll back into my head at the mere thought of how she'll taste. I already know it will be divine.

"Get started," she insists, driving me down by the shoulders until my mouth is level with the apex of her thighs. "It's finally time. Eat me, Big Boy," she demands.

CHAPTER 19

THEN

ALLISON WATCHES ME WITH SMOLDERING EYES, AND MY BREATH LEAVES ME completely. Never have better words been spoken.

Goddamn, I'm so ready for this.

As lightly as I can, I press my lips to the fabric of her thong, fluttering soft kisses along the length of her slit through the mesh. The exquisite scent of her arousal fills my nostrils and leaves my mouth watering in anticipation.

In a matter of moments, I'll have her spread out like a buffet, mine for the taking. But, she said to please her, and if it's the last thing I do, I'll make sure that's exactly what happens.

With deliberate slowness, I hook my fingers around the straps where her panties meet the round of her hips. Inch by inch, I drag the fabric down her thighs, trailing the tip of my tongue along the same path and providing the occasional nibble. Again, Allison's fingers weave their way into my hair, tugging faintly on the roots and sending tingles across my scalp.

Clearly, she likes to be bitten. Each time my teeth make contact with her delicate flesh, she swivels her hips in that direction.

Focusing on her face, on the way her lips part in anticipation, I retrieve the thong from around her ankles and toss it across the room. She looks down at me through those thick lashes, then curls her finger in my direction, summoning me.

Like an animal, I crawl back up her legs, only stopping when my mouth hovers right above her slick pussy. I suck on my finger, readying it for entry. Then, beginning at the apex of her thighs, I trail it down the length of her cunt. It glides so easily.

She's ready. Waiting.

Allison's moans are deafening when I plunge the digit into her molten center, pushing it in as far as her body will allow. Over and over, I finger her, adding a second, then a third, until my hand is wet with her juices. Her breathing hitches with every thrust, and as I pound into her tight little pussy, her ass lifts up off the mattress. The sight is a fucking marvel.

I never want it to stop. The glistening lubrication coating her cunt and now her ass is captivating. It sears itself into my memory, a moment of perfect bliss.

Unable to resist, I withdraw my hand and lick away the remnants of her excitement. She whimpers, begging me to start again. The salty and sweet slippery liquid coats my tongue, and it's the most delicious thing I've ever tasted. My heart lurches, and the world around me disappears.

She pulls on my strands, bringing my head closer to her sex.

There's only this. Me and Allison. This bed. Her fucking pussy. I'm going to demolish it, leave her quaking, render her legs useless, and have her gasping for air by the time I'm finished. I have no more restraint.

"Riley," she whispers.

Snatching her luscious hips, I jerk her toward me, then pin her thighs down against the bed. Once more feral, I lower my mouth to her cunt, dragging my tongue from her entrance to the peak of her swollen clit.

Allison cries out, thrilled by the sensation. Pinpricks of pain dot my skull as she grips my hair even tighter.

Need ignites me. Again, I lap up her irresistible pussy. Over and over, I drive my tongue inside of her, then slide back to the sensitive bundle of nerves at her pinnacle. Flicking. Swirling. Sucking. Nibbling. Adding my fingers into the mix. Pounding them into her without remorse. Again. Again. Again.

Each time I pause to catch my breath, Allison's hips rise to meet my lips, pressing her cunt into my face and grinding.

My free hand reaches for her heaving breasts, finding one of her rigid nipples and pinching it between my fingers. I roll the nub back and forth, tugging and playing until Allison can no longer stand it.

She cries out in absolute ecstasy as her orgasm rocks her frame. The inner walls of her pussy clench tightly around my fingers. Hot, wet cum drenches my face. As she moans, I continue my assault on her clit, milking every last bit of bliss from the explosion that I can.

The moment lasts an eternity, yet somehow, it's over too fast. I want her to cum again. Drown me in her slit. Suffocate me between those strong, malleable thighs. If she did, I'd die a happy man.

Gradually, the room falls silent as her moans and whimpers cease. I halt my barrage on her swollen clit, allowing her to pull me back up to her beautiful face. It's my turn to groan as she uses her thumb to wipe glistening liquid off my lower lip and licks the appendage clean. The hand still buried in my hair brings my mouth to hers, and our tongues tangle together like twining snakes.

Wrapping her powerful legs around me with ease that should not be possible, Allison uses her weight to flip me onto my back. Eager fingers make quick work of my pants. My boxers follow shortly after. Cool air caresses my skin, making me shiver.

Allison doesn't leave me waiting for long. Throwing one leg over my hips, she straddles me and hovers just above my cock. Heat generated from her arousal fills the short distance between us.

She's so close, yet so far away, and it takes everything I have not to seize her perfect ass and slam myself into her slit. My dick spasms, all too aware of the glory just out of reach. All eight inches of me are rigid as stone and angled straight toward her entrance.

Snatching me by the wrists, she pins my arms down against the mattress above my head, rendering them useless and opening my body to her every whim. As much as I want to, I don't try to fight her control. I just watch in awe as she lowers that sweet little cunt down, closer and closer, until it envelopes my tip.

"Fuck, Allison," I mutter when she pulls away, hovering again. "Don't tease me."

Allison tuts in mock disappointment before doing the exact same thing. "Shut your mouth, or I'll climb off of you and leave you all alone in my bed. Do you understand?"

I whimper. I actually fucking *whimper* when she lowers herself yet again, this time taking me deeper.

"God," I say. "More. Please, more. Please..."

"God isn't here with you, Riley," she hisses, answering my pleas and taking another inch. "He's never been to Wonderland. Poor man. No, it's just you and me, and if you're a very good boy, a very, *very* good boy, I'll show you all the sinful things he's been missing."

Finally, just as I can't stand it any longer, Allison seats herself fully on my erection, taking my entire cock, right down to the goddamn base. She waits, perfectly still, and digs her nails into the skin of my wrists while I try to remember how to breathe. It's harder than it's ever been, and I have zero fucking complaints.

When she moves again, her inner walls squeeze my shaft in all the right places. She swivels those fucking hips like a fallen angel, in circles and figure eights, then she crashes into me like a tidal wave, grinding her sensitive nub against my pelvis. I'm little more than her sex doll. All for her pleasure. A plaything, exactly as she'd said I'd be.

Allison leans closer to me, dangling her perky tits over my dumbstruck face. Her nipple grazes my lip, and she lets go of one of my wrists just long enough to force my mouth open, allowing me to capture it between my teeth. Undeniable desire has me sucking the soft nub, flicking and twirling my tongue over the turgid flesh.

Allison shudders, seemingly overcome by pleasure. Her body rocks. Up and down, back and forth, circles, and grinding again.

Losing myself to her ceaseless rhythm, I barely manage to hold myself together. My balls tighten, drawing closer and closer to my taint, desperate to cum, but I'm not ready.

I want this to last. I *need* this to last. I'm not some inexperienced schoolboy who can't control his own release.

Or, maybe I am. It's coming fast, and before I have time to think of something, anything else to distract me from the vixen riding me like a prized stallion, I'm right there, peering over the brink.

At some point, she releases her grasp on my arms and leans back, planting her palms above my knees. I have just enough time to take in the arch of her back, the slope of her stomach, and the way her tits sway as she fucks me senseless before she screams my name.

"Riley!"

That's all it takes. I'm undone, falling right off that cliff into oblivion.

My dick swells one last time, then pulses, My stomach muscles spasm, tightening and releasing. A wave of energy crashes through me, then drains from my body. Heat floods to my cheeks, and I let go, filling her tight little cunt with my hot seed.

Exhaustion like I've never felt settles over me when my orgasm ends, and I could swear Allison's skin glows faintly where it touches me. Those sometimes gold and sometimes crimson eyes flash with satisfaction. I can barely keep mine open, and my heart beats a sporadic samba in my chest.

My arms are jelly, and my legs don't even fucking exist. But, Allison seems unbothered by our efforts. She's not even winded, has barely broken a sweat. Meanwhile, I'm just a puddle of man lying in the center of her bed.

"Holy shit!" I spit, voice breathy and grating.

Allison slides off of my cock, then lays down beside me. She trails the tips of her fingers along my pecs and abs, eliciting a pleasurable tingling sensation, then circles the head of my dick. My body lurches with aftershocks, and she giggles.

"Was it worth it?" she asks.

"Fuck yeah," I answer. "Can we do that again?"

But, even as the words escape me, sleep calls to my entire being.

"Rest, Riley," she orders before pressing her swollen lips to mine. "I'm not done yet."

That's it. The world fades to black, and my body gives in to sleep.

CHAPTER 20

NOW

ANDREW DRAGS IN CHAIR. DOCTOR FOLLOWS. THEN, ANOTHER.

A man. Young. Handsome. Tall and clean cut. Strange expression.

Doctor sits by feet. Andrew stops by bed. Chair just out of reach.

Man pauses. Can't stop staring.

"Thank you, Andrew. Braxton, would you like to have a seat?"

Man is Braxton. Makes sense. Doctor retrieved him. Followed through. Didn't leave me. Not for long. Just like he said. Brought a... friend.

"I..." Braxton stalls. Shuffles feet. Hands in pockets. Looks around. "I don't know..."

"I can assure you, you are perfectly safe. Andrew is a capable guard, and Riley is on his best behavior today. There have been a few struggles since his arrival, but that's to be expected when a man is cornered and afraid. We all have a primal side to us that demands we do whatever we must to survive. Unfortunately for Riley, his has surfaced for his protection now and then."

Braxton watches Andrew. Andrew looks at me. Back to him. Silently agrees. Points to chair.

Braxton moves forward. Slowly sits. Gaze back on me. Mixed emotions. Fear. Sadness. Confusion.

"Riley, do you remember your friend?" Doctor inquires. Gestures toward Braxton.

Something in Braxton's face. It matches, but different. Same eyes. Same shape. Wrong expression. Should be... happy? No. Not happy. Proud? Confident. Relaxed. At ease.

Remember. Try to remember. Try so fucking hard. Search the corners of my mind. Dig deeper. Analyze posture. Clothes. Hair. Watch. Everything.

Head begins to ache.

"Maybe." All I can say. Not sure, but not unsure. Too vague. Lost in my mind. Searching for crumbs in smoky haze.

"Maybe is good," Doctor praises. "A place to start, yes?" Pats my leg. Smiles at Braxton. "We have a predicament on our hands, Braxton. See, Riley can't recall much of anything about how he has come to be in his current situation, I'm afraid. We're searching for answers together. So far, he has said some interesting things, which I would, of course, need his permission to disclose. If they become relevant, we can discuss them when the time comes. Thanks to your thorough description in your missing persons report, we've learned his identity. We've also discovered he has a fondness for pizza, which I will share because that doesn't seem too much like an invasion of his privacy."

Quiet chuckle. Surprises Braxton. Don't think he meant to do it. Glances at floor. Ashamed. Returns face to Doctor. "That's true. We order from the DoorMouse every game night. Always the same thing. Sausage and cheese. We had some that night before he disappeared."

"Did you?" Doctor asks. Reaches into shirt pocket. Withdraws a tiny notebook. Takes out pen. Clicks. Starts to scribble. "We were on the right track after all, Riley!" Pats leg again. "How about that?" Braxton confused. Doctor clarifies. "I thought the DoorMouse might be important to Riley's story, though I hadn't had the time yet to verify the guess. I'd intended to make a call after your visit this evening. It doesn't seem that will be necessary now."

DoorMouse. Sausage. Cheese. Pizza. Game night? Familiar. Friend?

What happened?

"Are you sports fans, Braxton?" Doctor asks. "You mentioned game night. Might there be a particular team Riley was passionate about?"

Braxton blinks rapidly. "Oh, not sports. Video games. Like, on the Xbox and PlayStation."

"I see. Thank you for that." Doctor writes more.

Shrugs shoulders. "O... Okay."

Doctor moves on. "Regardless, you were together the night he went missing. What can you tell us about that?"

"Right now?" Braxton asks.

"No time like the present," Doctor suggests.

"It's complicated," Braxton says. "I told the police about what happened. They should have everything you need."

Doctor frowns. Sympathetic. Questioning. "I've read the report, yes. But, I have a feeling there are things you didn't say when you spoke to the police. Things you may have hidden or intentionally omitted out of fear of the repercussions that might have followed such admissions."

Braxton squirms. "I don't know what you mean."

"I mean," Doctor continues, "that I am not a betting man, but I'd wager my next paycheck that you didn't simply enjoy a few drinks with your friend and head home for the night. Tell me, is that the full truth? Or perhaps, as I suspect, did you leave out a few details that might not have reflected upon yourself or your friend so kindly?"

Braxton looks at me. Looks for a long time. Considers answer. Gears turn in head. Guilty expression. Shame floods cheeks again.

"No, what I said isn't everything that happened."

What happened? Don't understand.

"Enlighten me, then." Doctor studies Braxton. Waits patiently, then adds, "Braxton, I am not the police. I am not here to punish you for

121

your sins. I'm here for Riley, as are you. What needs to happen now is complete honesty. Without the information you're withholding, I may not be able to help your friend, but with it, we can open doors and find answers."

Open doors… Key.

Braxton sighs. Hesitates. Shoulders drop. Worry lines on forehead and around eyes. Mouth twitches.

"Riley has had a rough go of it lately," he confesses. "His fiancée cheated on him. She left him not too long ago, and he's been depressed ever since. So, I came over and suggested that he leave the house. I wanted to help him get over her, you know?"

"I do," Doctor agrees. "Might I ask, who is this departed fiancée?"

"Her name is Celeste. Celeste March. She's back with her ex. I think they're on vacation. When I went looking for Riley, I reached out to her, but I never heard back. I'm not sure where they are, exactly. Her Insta is full of pictures of the two of them in the tropics sharing oysters and whatever. You ask me, I think he looks like a walrus. Big buck teeth. Fat face. I don't know what she sees in him. She's crazy." Braxton winces. "Sorry, I just mean that Riley deserves better."

"Alright. I gather you and I will not find much assistance from Miss Celeste. That's a shame." Doctor draws heavy line on paper. Strikes through name. "We can cross her off the list, then. Tell me about your evening together. You came over to cheer Riley up, and off to the bar you went?"

"Yes. I mean, sort of. Well, it wasn't really a bar. More like a club? I'd been there a few times before. There's a dance floor, and they serve drinks. I thought he might find someone to…" Trails off.

"Fuck," Doctor finishes. Tone at ease.

Andrew laughs. Leans against far wall.

Braxton shies away. Flinches. "That's one way to put it." Cheeks flame red.

"There is research that suggests finding a new partner can be *very* beneficial for the broken hearted," Doctor offers. "Coitus is healthy for the body and mind. There's no shame in that. You may not have been too far off base in your attempts to aid your friend."

Braxton's expression lightens. Less embarrassed. "I only wanted to help. I figured there was no reason to hole himself up away from the rest of the world and mope. So yeah, we went to the club."

"Go on," Doctor insists.

"I didn't stay for too long, though. There was a girl, and she invited me back to her place. Shit, I shouldn't have left him there, but he seemed totally fine. I didn't know. She was hot, and I was horny, so I gave Riley some money for the tab and left."

"Interesting." Doctor writes another note. "Do you remember the name of the club you visited?"

Braxton thinks. Frowns. "Something about a rabbit. I didn't pay that much attention. It's one of those hole-in-the-walls in a back alley. No sign or anything. I only knew about it because one of the girls I hooked up with loved the place."

Doctor turns to me. Clicks pen. Ponders Braxton's answer. "Curiouser and curiouser."

"What is?" Braxton asks.

"Some of the pieces are beginning to fall into place. Riley has been trying to convey information about a rabbit, though in his condition, he finds himself incapable of forming coherent sentences. I am not sure if he's able to structure his thoughts efficiently." Doctor shakes head. "That's putting it kindly. Let me rephrase. I know he isn't. But, he's trying, and he's getting closer. Many of the others have dismissed his words as nonsensical madness, but I've been paying attention."

A club. Flashing lights. Loud music. Dark shadows. People. So many people. Everywhere. Stale air and sex.

"Your friend has spoken several times about following a rabbit."
Doctor considers. Turns back to Braxton. Clicks pen again. "Perhaps, it
has to do with the name of the establishment?"

Braxton's forehead scrunches. Lips thin. "There… there was a logo on
Dynah's cup. Hold on."

"Dynah?"

"The girl I left with."

"You wouldn't have happened to get her last name, would you?"
Doctor muses.

"Not a chance. I'm sorry." Braxton grimaces.

"That's alright." Doctor smiles. Reassures. "I assumed such would
likely be the case. In my experience, sexual conquests usually do not
lead to long-term commitments."

Braxton nods. Reaches around. Pulls phone out from back pocket.
Types something. Can't see.

Stares at phone. Scrolls. Scrolls. Scrolls. Finally, smiles. Passes device to
Doctor.

Doctor squints at screen. "Is this the logo you recall?"

"I think so."

"The Rabbit Hole?"

"That sounds right," Braxton confirms.

Compulsion commands me. "Pretty rabbit," I mumble. Words flow
freely. "Follow. Pretty Rabbit."

Doctor scribbles again. "Seeing as though we've earned a response
from Riley, I'd say you were correct. Thank you, Braxton."

"Late. Blue Poison. Down the hatch," I add. Head lolls to side. Close
eyes. Try to focus. To stop speaking. Listen. Learn.

So hard. Exhausting.

Want to sleep. Keep resisting.

"Do those words mean anything to you?" Doctor asks.

"No," Braxton replies. Runs hands through hair. "I only know which club we went to. Honestly, I want to help, but like I said, I left pretty quickly."

Doctor taps pen on chin. "Please, don't disregard your ability to assist Riley. I wasn't with you that evening, and yet, there are many things I can do to help guide you friend back to stability. You may still be of use in other ways. For example, can you tell me whether Riley partakes in recreational drugs?"

Open eyes. Interested.

Do I?

Braxton withdraws. Doesn't respond.

"Let me remind you that I'm not the police, Braxton. I simply need answers."

"Weed," he admits. Reluctant. "He smokes. I mean, *we* smoke. Not all the time but every once and a while."

"Yes, there were traces of Marijuana in Riley's system. That's not uncommon, especially for a man of his age. What I meant was, does Riley dabble in anything stronger? Anything that might have impaired his mental state?"

"Never." Braxton's firm. "Nothing like that. We did Molly once in college at a music festival. It wasn't his thing. He likes to be in control of himself."

"I see." Doctor pauses. "You say you left money for the tab. Is he a heavy drinker, by chance?"

"Not usually."

"Not usually?"

Braxton cringes. "I might have influenced his behavior. I thought if he got wasted, it would be easier for him to move on from Celeste. So, I told him to drink until he couldn't remember." Head falls into hands. He groans. "Fuck, do you think this is my fault? It is, isn't it? I should have stayed with him."

"Braxton, unless you've injured your friend, this is not your doing," Doctor responds. "You must keep that in mind. Guilt is a vicious thing. It taints a person, not unlike poison. We can't have that. Not now. Riley needs you at your best. He can't afford for you to spend your time wallowing in self-pity."

"But, I left him there. I was a shit friend."

"To some extent, yes. We are, all of us, capable of imperfect choices. As for your friend, Riley is a man with free will, and more than likely, he did as he pleased, regardless of your instructions. So did his assailant. You did not break him. You are not the reason he is in this bed. Not unless you're hiding some terrible misdeed, and I don't believe that to be the case."

Braxton sighs. "If you say so."

"What about potential partners?" Doctor continues. "Before you left the club, had he shown an interest in anyone?"

"Only the bartender," Braxton admits. "She was smoking hot. I sort of challenged him to take her home with him." Embarrassment returns. "As far as I could tell, it wasn't gonna happen. That chick was over our shit before we even walked into the place. I was kind of a dick, and since he came with me, she wasn't having it."

"Hmm." Doctor scratches chin. "And, was anyone particularly aggressive toward your friend?"

"Nobody. Not while I was there."

"Okay, then. You've given me a great deal to consider, Braxton. I'll have to think on what you've told me tonight. Truly, I appreciate your candor in spite of the circumstances."

Braxton straightens. Blows out a breath. Watches me with concern.

"Can you fix him?" he asks.

Sadness. So much sadness. Washes off both. Doctor is consumed.

"I'm going to try. We all are. Let's take it one step at a time. Riley's facing a difficult road. It's possible he can overcome his struggles, but we will have to be patient with him."

"Fix me," I whisper.

Missing. Broken. Terrified. Defeated.

The room is silent. They watch me. I watch them.

"Is there any way I could spend a moment alone with him?" Braxton asks.

Doctor scratches chin. Folds up notebook. Tucks into pocket. Deposits pen.

"That would be…" he begins. Searches for words. "Unconventional, given the circumstances. May I ask why?"

"To apologize," Braxton says. "I owe him that much, even if you're right and this is not my fault."

Doctor looks at Andrew. Andrew looks at me. Braxton studies exchange.

"I have to warn you that Riley has had a few violent outbursts during his stay. To leave you alone with him in this state would be to put you in danger. I'm not sure —"

"I can sign a waiver or whatever," Braxton interrupts. "I'm not afraid of him. He won't hurt me. And even if he did, I would deserve it. I'm not gonna sue you or anything. Please?"

Pregnant pause. Andrew shakes head. Narrows eyes at Doctor. Scoffs. Shakes head again.

Doctor studies tile. Picks at nails.

"How long do you need?" Doctor asks.

"Not long."

"I can't give you much time."

"Five minutes?"

Andrew frowns. "This is not a good idea, Doctor Barrows. You saw what he was like before. The patient is a liability. Doctor Gates will haul you in front of the board if this goes south. You'll lose your job and your license."

No one speaks.

Doctor stands. Too still. Unsure. Torn.

Finally, makes choice. Hand on Braxton's shoulder. Glance at me.

Heads toward Andrew. Stops at door.

"Five minutes," he says, "and Andrew will be just outside. Understood?"

"Crystal clear," Braxton replies.

"Be careful with him. You have more than one life in your hands."

Doctor leaves. Takes Andrew with him.

CHAPTER 21
THEN

"WAKE UP, BIG BOY."

Allison's command pulls me from a deep and dreamless sleep. Her voice sounds tinny and muffled by distance. It's just the lingering pull of the void, though. Struggling, I will consciousness to return. My eyes beg me to remain dormant, resisting even as I force them open.

I've never been this exhausted before. Allison fucked me into oblivion.

I can already tell I'm not yet in control of my senses. My body, still reeling from all of the drinks, is heavier than it should be and uncomfortably numb. My extremities are ghosts of themselves, there but not there, tingling with pins and needles. A dull headache is beginning in the center of my forehead. My head lolls to the side, neck unwilling to hold up the damn thing.

There's no telling how long I was asleep. It could have been a few minutes or it could have been a few hours. I was lost to the world. Completely gone.

Groggily, I try to scan the room, searching for her. Confusion outweighs the drowsiness as I realize I can't see. There should be a window over there, and I know we came through a door on the far wall, but they're nowhere to be found. Everything is dark. Pitch black. It's like I'm trapped in a room that doesn't exist.

She must have turned off the neon lights that cast her bedroom in that sultry glow. Maybe they keep her awake? That would make sense. I don't sleep with my lights on at home. Why would she?

But, I'm not familiar enough with the space to feel at ease. I didn't arrange the furniture. I don't belong here. I'm just a stranger passing through her life, a lost puppy dog that followed her home from a back alley.

"Riley," she calls again. Her voice is closer this time. There's a seductive quality to her tone like she's teasing me. "I said I wasn't done with you yet. I knew you were breakable, but I didn't think you'd give up so easily."

Allison's fingers trail, featherlite, across one of my shoulders and down my arm. Where her skin touches mine, heat blooms, reminding me of sunburn. She stops when she reaches my forearm, retreating. Then, she unexpectedly cups my balls, sending a spark of arousal to my core with a squeeze.

Surprised, I let out a groan. My body stiffens. So does my dick.

"There he is," she whispers, mouth close to my ear. Allison's hot breath gives me a shiver, raising goosebumps along my bare skin. "Welcome back to Wonderland. You've been missed."

Thinking I'd be able to capture her mouth with mine, I turn my head to the side, searching for her pouty lips. She's not there, but the motion comes with a realization — something silky covers my forehead and cheekbones.

A pillow? No, that's not right. It doesn't have the weight. My eyes roll back into my head and I blow out a breath. It's a blindfold, then. She's stolen my vision. But, when did she put it on, and how had she done so without waking me?

I've never been blindfolded before. Everything Celeste and I did was so vanilla. Missionary or cowgirl. Nothing too exciting. Not my choice. Hers. I'd always been up for more adventurous activities. Celeste wasn't. Every time I brought up the idea of trying something new, more sensual, she shut me down. Eventually, I gave up and accepted what she offered because I loved her, or I thought I did.

Allison is anything but vanilla. She's an explosion of flavor. If I'm lucky, she'll teach me a few new tricks.

She already is.

Unconsciously, I attempt to raise my hand to my face to touch the slippery silk. Another surprise awaits me when I'm unable to do so, met with a sudden jolt and a tight pressure around my wrist. Shifting my feet, I find them similarly bound in her devilish trap. She has me in restraints. Leather cuffs, if I had to guess. The bands are wide, and the edges of them bite into my flesh.

Again, I'm impressed with her skill. I'm a notoriously light sleeper. I must have blacked out and been dead to the world. Otherwise, she has *very* deft fingers.

Increasing discernment works its way through me. I become acutely aware of the chill in the air and the lack of blankets underneath me. In fact, most of my backside is exposed. I'm not on the bed at all. A hard surface presses against the soles of my feet.

I don't know how, but I'm standing, arms and legs spread wide. My body dangles like a scarecrow from something solid. Something wooden. Something…

The cross… the one I'd seen in the corner when I walked in. She's moved me and tressed me up on the sturdy frame.

How the fuck?

"Allison?" I let my head fall back into empty air, confirming my suspicion. My voice is raspy, my throat dry. "What's going on?"

"What's the matter?" she croons from my other side.

Her hands explore my naked thighs, climbing ever higher, coming so close but yet never to where I want them to be.

Fucking tease.

"I thought you wanted to play?"

"I do, but — "

"But, nothing," she interrupts. "We have a deal. I took you home, gave you the night of your dreams, and now I get to use you."

"How did you — " I don't get to finish my thought. Allison grips my chin and forces my lips apart, then shoves a bit between them before I manage to spit out the words. She makes quick work of the ribbon it's attached to, tying it behind my head. "Mfmm r doo?" I hear myself say. It was supposed to be "What the fuck are you doing?" but the gag makes it impossible to speak.

She's stolen my sight and my voice, the little vixen.

"I'm having fun," she answers cooly, deciphering my question with practiced ease. She's done this before. I shouldn't be surprised. "And, if you can follow directions, you will be, too. Be a good boy now, Riley. Stay quiet, and I'll let you cum. Be a naughty boy, and there will be consequences. Think you can handle that?"

Swallowing, I nod my head. *Hell yes,* I think, hoping to God she can read my thoughts.

"Excellent." Before I realize what she's doing, Allison stuffs plugs into my ears, blocking out all sound except for my thrumming heartbeat.

Blindfolded, gagged, deafened, and restrained, I'm helpless, entirely at her mercy. The only indication of her movements is the faint reverberation of her footsteps as she crosses the room, leaving me alone, naked and vulnerable.

She said she likes her men weak. This must be what she meant.

My cock hardens in anticipation. Even though I know it won't make a difference, I strain to listen. My pulse increases, and every nerve in my body comes to life, desperate for her return.

Seconds later, a stinging pain assaults my abs, the bite of a riding crop smacking my skin. It catches me off guard and I jump, tugging against my restraints. The cuffs hold firm, and the cross keeps me in place.

Smack! The biting sensation comes again, this time on my chest. She targets my nipples, over and over, then moves to the slope of my neck.

Smack! Smack! Each consecutive impact is harder, more brutal. Repeatedly, she swats my inner thighs and ass. My dick throbs with every hit.

Smack! My forearm… my pecs my ribs.

"Fwuck," I grunt, grinding my teeth into the bit. "Mmmf." My flesh burns like fire at the site of every place the crop has touched. Pleasure mixes with pain, intense and consuming.

Abruptly, the attack ceases. Allison withdraws, leaving my flesh alive and tingling.

What is she doing now? Where has she gone? Probably searching for another toy. I can only imagine the depraved things she's going to do to me.

I'm so focused on the fading flames licking my body that I don't realize she's returned before she appears behind me. She threads her slender fingers through my hair, grabbing a healthy fistful. The roots protest as she yanks my head back and presses a harsh kiss against my cheek. Then, she releases me.

Anticipation builds. I can't tell where she's gone. She could be right next to me or in the next building.

I don't have to wait long for my answer.

Allison squeezes my hips, then slowly drags her fingers down the length of my legs, leaning her body weight against me and lowering herself to the floor. From there, she lets them wander up my inseam, skating over my calves and knees. Paying special attention to my thighs, she kisses and nibbles her way toward my groin but always keeps her touch just out of range.

Without warning, she presses something firm and cool to the underside of my cock and simultaneously gives it one good lick, right on the tip.

An intense vibration begins where she bears down on the unidentified toy, shocking me and making me squirm with frenzied need.

"Mmmf," I exclaim again as tension coils rapidly within me. Allison rolls the vibrator up and down my length. At the rate she's going, this won't last more than a minute. My abs are already clenching, and I can feel the precipice nearing. "Fwuck. Fwuck meh…"

I drive my cock against the toy, begging for more stimulation, but Allison takes it away, and the soul-crushing vacancy leaves me panting.

The intensity subsides. I struggle to catch my breath.

Then, she begins her games once again. Unyielding. Relentless.

Over and over, Allison brings me to the edge before pulling back at exactly the last second. My dick twitches, begging for release, and yet I know she has no intention of giving it.

Start. Stop. Start. Leave me pleading. Weak in the knees. Aching for her touch.

She cradles my balls, massaging them as the sensation builds.

It's getting harder and harder to breathe.

Suddenly, Allison abandons her toy and grabs my dick with both of her hands, then lowers her mouth to its base. I cry out in pleasure as she starts at the bottom, languidly dragging her tongue up to the tip. She flicks the moist muscle against the point where my head meets my shaft, focusing on that delicious, sensitive spot that makes me want to drive my cock down her throat, then wraps those sexy little lips around my crown.

My chest heaves with desire as she cleans away my arousal, savoring the drops that have seeped out already. I can't hear her, but I can feel her moan against my member before she pulls away, then brings her mouth back to my shaft.

Fuck, I wish I could see what she's doing. I want to remember the way her plump lips wrap around my cock. I want to watch as her saliva coats my member. I want to see her swallow me completely, pumping me into her mouth until I'm at the edge of pleasure and pain. I want to see my seed explode onto her tongue and drip down her chin.

But, I can't. It's a special form of torture. One I can't say I hate, either. Without my sight, every touch is amplified. Every lick makes me jerk against my bonds. Every suck makes me quiver with need. I'm all nerves and frenzy and hunger. My pleasure is her will, and I owe my life to the goddess on her knees.

She could save me, or she could destroy me, and right now, neither option could be sweeter.

For these moments, I am hers. I am nothing. I am no one. My name, my life, my body, my world — all are completely forgotten.

Allison lets go of my dick and presses her palms to my ass, gripping my glutes tight enough to leave bruises. Her nails bite into my flesh, surely leaving perfect crescents where they've broken the skin.

"Uuuhhhff," I whimper as Allison pulls away. Her absence leaves me feeling far too empty. The heat of her mouth is replaced with ice as air settles against my skin where her tongue had been.

I want it back. I want her on her knees again — now. Need it. Crave it. Can't think of anything else.

Minutes turn to hours as I wait, praying for her attention. She's doing it on purpose. Dragging it out. Filling me with insatiable desire.

Suddenly, the blindfold is torn away.

The neon lights are back. Left in darkness for too long, my eyes refuse to focus, making everything blurry. Still, my goddess stands before me, stark naked and oh so blissfully eager. Her nipples pebble on those perfect fucking breasts. Moisture slickens her inner thighs. Lust pierces through her crimson eyes like daggers. She tilts her head with a wicked grin, then takes the plugs out of my ears, bringing back the sounds of the world.

After the pain and pleasure and deprivation, all of the sensations are overwhelming.

"How does it feel?" Allison asks me, pressing her supple frame flat against mine. She tips her head back and licks my bottom lip.

My mouth falls open, ready to return the favor if it weren't for the gag. The damn thing is in the way.

I can't kiss her, and I can't answer her. She knows that. She doesn't want me to. She wants to torture me, and holy shit is she good at it.

Allison pulls away and nuzzles her nose along my jaw. Instinct has me reaching for her, but she hasn't undone the restraints that bind my arms, either. I'm still at her mercy.

"You've behaved better than I expected," she continues. "So, I gave you back your sight. I'm going to let you see yourself explode. Do you want that, Riley? Do you want to watch?"

The cross creaks as I nod my head like there's no tomorrow.

My vision begins to clear as I blink away the fog. Allison, a sight to behold, trails sweet kisses along my pecs and my abs, lowering herself back to the ground, inch by inch. The little white bow she'd been wearing is gone. Her blonde hair hangs freely past her shoulders, tickling my skin as she goes. I'm struck by an urge to grab fistfuls of it as she likes to do to mine. My hands spasm at the thought, then go still when I notice something new.

In place of that innocent little white bow are a pair of tiny, ivory horns, angling away from her face like handlebars. They look remarkably real. I'm impressed despite myself.

Fuck, she wants to roleplay, huh? She must have dug out an old Halloween costume while I slept. I can get behind that, though I'd much rather get behind her.

A vision of me burying my cock inside of her tight little pussy again while I grip her hips and slam into her repeatedly fills my thoughts. Allison senses my growing arousal and pauses, blowing hot air over my shaft, making it jump. My breath hitches, and my fingers itch to wrap around her prosthetics, to steer her mouth back to my dick and shove it down her throat.

"Do you like them?" she asks. Allison prods at the tips of the protrusions and hovers inches away from my groin.

I do. God, I fucking love them. She's so unpredictable. So different. I needed this in my life. Needed her.

"Yessh," I answer, forcing my words out around the bit.

"Good," she replies. Lust fills Allison's gaze.

The corner of her mouth lifts into a temptatious smile, then her lips part. She presses her palms to my inner thighs and squeezes. Her head dips down, and she grazes my crown with her tongue, the faintest touch. Straightening her spine, she stares up at me with mischievous eyes. When she licks her lips, the sight stops my heart.

A forked tongue, not unlike that of a snake's, skates across her swollen mouth. When it reaches the corner, the reptilian muscle flicks before disappearing. She blinks and cocks her head, daring me to say a single word.

Even if I could talk, I'd be speechless. Denial floods through me.

This isn't real. It can't be. But, fuck if those gorgeous, impossible, crimson eyes aren't slitted.

"How about my tongue?" she inquires, looking up at me through her lashes. "Do you like that, too?"

My eyes widen, and my startled body catches up to my vision, trying and failing to shove itself backward, away from her.

There's nowhere to go. The wooden cross presses into my shoulder blades and hips, reminding me that I'm caught in her trap like a fly in a spider's web.

I swallow hard, willing my intoxicated brain to search for answers, to figure out what the fuck is going on.

Allison watches me with fervent interest as I struggle to accept the only rational excuse my mind offers, that my eyes are playing tricks on me.

It was a hallucination. Had to be. A freaky fucking hallucination. God, I must be drunker than I'd thought.

"You have no idea what you've gotten yourself into, do you?" she teases. "Innocent little Riley. The nice guy with the douchey friend. The one with the broken heart."

Her forked tongue makes another appearance, flicking again, this time too close to my dick for comfort. It's too real, too long and thin, too perfect to be a hallucination. Fear seeps into my bones, and I recoil.

"Oh, don't be like that," she says. "I tried to warn you, you know. I gave you chances. Chester did, too. I heard the two of you talking outside of the club. But, you didn't want to hear it, did you? Didn't want to back off."

Allison averts her gaze, withdrawing one hand and admiring her fingers under the dim light. Mesmerized by the impossible, I watch as the digits lengthen. No, not her fingers. Her nails. Once cut short, they grow, reshaping into honed talons — thick, black, and sharp.

All at once, survival instinct kicks in. Springing to action, I strain against my bindings, tugging on my wrists and ankles. The cuffs hold, showing no sign of weakening, and so does the cross.

It's no use. I'm strong but not *that* strong. Not like this. Not when I'm held aloft.

Allison drags one of her talons from the back of my knee up to my balls. A thin trail of blood follows where the tip carves into my flesh. A scream of fury and horror tears free from my throat. She licks the drop off of her claw and groans, thoroughly pleased.

"It's too late to fight me now," she adds, placing her hand back down on my thigh. The touch burns like hellfire, no longer pleasant. "My venom courses through your veins. Has since you were back at The Rabbit Hole. I laced the drinks, and you devoured every last drop, didn't you? So greedy. You were mine before you stepped out into that alley, and you didn't even know it."

She points one of her talons at my tip but doesn't touch it. I can't look away, terrified of what she's planning to do.

"Who are we kidding? You were mine the moment you sat down at my bar."

Allison wraps her deadly hands around my cock, and I still.

"And, every time you kissed me, every second you spent tasting my cunt, increased the dose." She rolls her neck. Silky blonde hair grazes my leg. "I almost wish you were an asshole, you know? Because assholes are like appetizers. A dime a dozen. Never enough to satiate you, but plenty to get the party started."

Allison begins to pump my dick, squeezing and letting go, varying her pressure like a goddamn pro.

"You should have been more like that other one. The one you came with. What was his name? Whatever. It doesn't matter. I might have taken someone else home tonight if you were. Wayne would have been thrilled to join me. But, that's not who you are, is it? You're a good man. A nice one. Good men are special. Delectable. Rare. How could I resist?"

She flicks her tongue again.

"Hhuupp," I cry, desperate for someone to hear me.

They won't. Allison is too smart. Her home is too vast. I'd have thought it insane before, but now I'm convinced it's a pocket dimension. Besides, my pleas are muffled by the gag. There's no chance in hell anyone is coming to my aid, even if it isn't. Not at this hour. Not in a place like this.

"Appetizers leave you disappointed," she continues. "Good men leave you satisfied. Stuffed."

Fuck you, I think. *You fucking bitch! You demonic whore!*

Allison tuts. "Your thoughts are filthy, Riley. There's no need for that. I like dirty talk as much as the rest of them, but that was just uncalled for."

My eyes widen when I realize she can hear my inner monologue.

Devilishness contorts Allison's gorgeous features. "We still have time before dawn," she adds. She increases the speed of her movements. Against all odds, my dick is still rock-hard. With practiced ease, she rubs the pad of her thumb along the sensitive flesh on the bottom up to the sweet spot. Tension coils in my stomach, an automatic reaction.

"Relax," Allison commands. "It will be far worse for you if you struggle." A whimper escapes me as she strokes my shaft. "I'd rather do this the easy way than the hard way." Her pace increases, filling my dick with a familiar electric hum. "It's your choice, though. If you'd rather make things difficult, you can. Either way, I'm hungry, and I will get what I want."

Allison moves her hands to my ass and squeezes, digging her talons into my glutes. Her forked tongue shoots out and coils around my dick, pulsing. She takes all of me into her mouth, deep into her throat, sucking me until I'm nearly senseless.

Horror and revulsion overcome me as my pleasure builds.

Just before an orgasm can rip through me, Allison releases me, letting the feeling crest and plateau. Her tongue withdraws, disappearing behind her lips. "Your fear makes you sweeter," she coos. "Every time you shatter for me, it makes harvesting your soul that much easier." When she smiles again, fanged teeth spark under the neon glow. "Fight all you want, Big Boy. Plead for your freedom. No one is coming. You're all alone."

Making one more effort to escape, I yank on my cuffs, trying to tear them free from the cross. They don't budge.

"I told you," Allison begins. I watch in disgust as a tail sprouts from her lower back, wrapping itself up my leg and winding toward my ass. "I eat guys like you for dinner." It brushes the cleft where my cheeks touch. She strokes the appendage lovingly. "They never last until the morning."

CHAPTER 22

NOW

ROOM IS QUIET. BRAXTON UNCOMFORTABLE. NERVOUS. KEEPS GLANCING over shoulder. Waiting for door to open. Expression odd. Fearful. Reminds me of child keeping watch for adult.

Has trouble looking at me. Catch him glancing. Immediately turns away.

Can't stand to see me. Why not? Supposed to be friend. Doesn't make sense.

Braxton places hands in lap. Knees bounce. Shake his arms. Fidgets with watch. Picks at cuticles. Skin grows raw. Beads with blood. Doesn't wince. Stares hole in wall.

Braxton thinks. Doesn't speak. Not at first. Being careful. Choosing right words.

Are there right words? Why so hard?

Takes several minutes. Opens mouth. Closes again. Abandons picking. Runs fingers through hair. Furrows brow.

"I'm sorry," he mumbles. Voice low. Sad and regretful. "This is all my fault."

Tilt head to side. Consider him. Wait for more.

"You didn't want to go out. I convinced you to go with me. I picked the club. I left you alone so I could hook up with a random drunk chick. Those were my choices, not yours, and look where they've gotten you."

Choices. He made choices. *Did I?* Wanted to stay home. Didn't want to leave. Can't remember why. Can't remember home.

"Fuck, man" Braxton continues. "I'm a shit friend and a shit person." Face falls.

Braxton is broken. Just like me, but also different. Haunted eyes. Slumped shoulders. So much pain.

Pain.

I know pain. Stinging begins again. Spurred on by anxiety. Restraints. First in feet. Below cuffs. Creeps up legs. Inches toward waist. Pricks arms.

"I didn't mean to be," he admits. "You have to know that. Do you know that, Riley?"

Do I? No. I don't.

Braxton is familiar. Know his face. Recall his voice. Doctor says Braxton is friend.

But, I don't know him. Not all. Only pieces.

"I should have known better than to take you to The Rabbit Hole. There are so many clubs in the city, and I picked the hole-in-the-wall with the shit reputation. What a fucking joke. What was I thinking?"

Reputation? For what? Bad feeling. Don't like this. Feels wrong.

Tightness in chest. Heart beats faster. Breaths grow shallow. Dry swallow.

"Oh, who am I kidding?" Braxton asks. Not asking me. Asking himself. "I know what I was thinking. I'm fucking lying to myself."

Lying. Lies. Liar. Tricks.

Danger.

Liars hurt. Tricksters kill.

Muscles strain in arms.

Bad friend. Bad person.

Bad Braxton.

"I wouldn't have even known about The Rabbit Hole if it weren't for Celeste. That's the kicker, isn't it? I wasn't totally honest with the Doctor earlier. It wasn't a chick I hooked up with who showed me the place. It was her, man."

Celeste. Said name before. To Doctor. Fiancée.

My fiancée. Not anymore. Left me. Broke heart. Drove me to her.

Braxton pales. Eyes start to water. Hands tremble. Frowns.

"When Celeste dumped you, she chewed your ass up and spit you out like it was nothing. That bitch. It wasn't right. The worst part is I could have done something about it, but I was too busy worrying about hurting you to open my goddamn mouth."

Chewed. Biting. Gnashing. Gnawing. Teeth in flesh. Ripping. Rending. Devouring.

No... no... no no no no no no!

She's back. In my head. Crawling over me. Skin on skin. Nails sinking deep. Drawing blood. Teeth too sharp. At my throat. Gouging. Tearing...

Body shivers. Stomach churns.

"I knew Celeste was cheating on you. I fucking knew about it. I could have told you, and I kept my stupid mouth shut." Pauses. Deep breath. Regret. "You don't remember, but a week or so before she called the wedding off, you guys had a huge argument. It was so dumb. Who gives a shit about which flowers go in the bouquets? I don't know. Girls, I guess? But, she stormed out of your place, and you called me, and we chilled for hours at your apartment. She didn't come back until three in the morning. And when she did, she smelled like some other asshole's cologne. I couldn't let that stand. So, I went to her work the next day, and I followed her when she got off."

Finally looks at me. Locks eyes. They're too hard. Steel. Stone.

"She wasn't even hiding it. That's the thing. She went straight for the parking garage and hopped into the douche's car. Celeste didn't even check to see if she was alone. She just tore into him. Ripped his clothes off and straddled his lap right there."

Tore... Tore... Tore.

"I took pictures for proof, and when he left her there, I cut her off before she made it back to her ride. That bitch didn't even flinch. She laughed when I confronted her. Laughed so goddamn hard. I told her I'd show them to you if she didn't tell you what was going on. Gave her a week. She just flipped me off and drove away."

Braxton stops. Eyes go distant. Lost in memory. Shakes head. Scoffs.

"I've never hit a woman, but if she'd been a dude, I'd have laid her the fuck out." Rage bunches muscles. He flexes hands. Grinds jaw. "I hoped she'd do the right thing, but she didn't. I should have told you. You could have ended things on your terms, not hers. Maybe you wouldn't have been so broken. Maybe we never would have gone to The Rabbit Hole."

'I like broken men.' Her voice in my ear. Sends terror down spine. Lungs seize. Breaths grow shallow.

"I followed her again a few nights later, and she met the douche at The Rabbit Hole. That's how I found it."

Rabbit Hole. Follow the rabbit. Down the hatch. Drink me. Blue poison.

Eyes roll back. See it in my head. Hear it. Flashing lights. Booming music. Blue drink. Cocktail napkin. Mushrooms...

"Eat me," I whisper.

"I'd be pissed at me, too." Braxton leans forward. Head in hands. Calm at first. Then, growls. "She didn't stay at The Rabbit Hole long. Maybe like an hour. But, I went inside and watched them. The place had good drinks. I knocked a few back. Good snacks, too. And fuck, there were tons of people on the dance floor. So, when I took you out, I figured why not? Celeste wasn't gonna show up. She was too busy with Mallick. As far as I could tell, that place was stocked with desperate pussy. I figured you had a better shot of getting laid and getting over her ass so you could start acting like yourself again if we hit up the club."

"Down the hatch." Fists so tight. Knuckles whiten. Arms strain against bonds. Head rolls. Ears pound.

Stinging more intense. Wasps crawling on stomach. On chest. Burrowing. Pinching. Stabbing.

Too much. Too much. Make it stop. Make it stop… Please… please, no. No more.

"You've always been the nice one. The good guy, you know? The one who'd do anything for anyone? I mean, shit, you put up with me. Anytime I needed you, there you were. Reliable Riley. My best friend."

'You're a good man. A nice one. Good men are special. Delectable. Rare.'

Skull fills with echoes. Fragments. Memories just below surface.

'Good men leave you satisfied. Stuffed.'

Words just like his. Too close.

Adrenaline surges. Flush hot. Sweat beads brow.

Danger.

He took me to her.

No doctor here. No help. No one but Braxton. But me.

Cornered.

Can't run.

Focus. Listen. Watch. Absorb.

Hear his words. Might save me. Might keep him at bay. Keep him away. Just for a while. Just long enough.

Suddenly, Braxton yells. Pushes to feet. Shoves chair away. Screeching noise. Metal grinding on floor. Heavy steps.

Angry. Violent.

Too fucking close! Too loud! Too much!

Head splits. Right down center. Searing agony. Vision clouds. Lose focus.

Can't see. Can't see him. Can't defend.

Lamb to the slaughter.

Easy target. Weak. Prey.

Buzzing. Buzzing. Stinging. Crawling. Creeping. Piercing. Under skin now. In mouth. Over eyelids.

Braxton paces.

"I let her break you. If you had been the one to end things with Celeste, maybe you wouldn't have been so damn mopey. Maybe I wouldn't have needed to drag you out to the bar. Maybe you would have been okay. I don't know, maybe not. But like, how was I supposed to know? And, I hated it. Hated seeing you so fucked up. So, I just wanted to make it right, and then I went and ruined your goddamn life."

Ruined life. Ruined. Destroyed…

His fault.

"And the best part is, my dumbass called Celeste thinking she would care that you were missing because you guys were together for so long. Nice, huh? Real smart, considering how she left things. You know what she said? Fucking bitch. She told me she hoped someone found you in a ditch on the side of the road. Man, she's something else. Hollow. I don't know what you ever saw in her."

Braxton chuckles. Mirthless. Cold.

"But, you don't even remember. None of it. Not her. Not me. That's the worst part. Because I want to be pissed at Celeste, but she didn't drag you to the club. I did. And, I want to be pissed at you for going missing, but I don't even know what the hell happened. So, how can I? I mean, look at yourself. What the fuck, Riley? What happened to you? Nobody has answers. And, I can tell you all of this shit, apologize until I'm blue in the face, but you can't forgive me because you don't even fucking know me, dude."

Braxton curls hand into fist. Slams it into wall.

"Aarraagh!" He screams. Furious. "None of this is right. None of it. Not what she did to you. Not what I did to you. Not what this is doing to me. None of it. None of it! Jesus, I'm so fucking sorry."

Braxton moves. Too fast. Too close to bed.

Knuckles raw. Scraped. Exposed.

Bloody.

Considers me. Blows out breath. Falls to knees. Extends arm. Reaches for my shoulder.

No! Scream in mind. Can't make words come. Can't control lips. Tongue. *No. No! Don't. Don't do it. Don't touch me! Don't hurt me. Get… get away! Get out!*

Clasps my joint. Squeezes. Too much. Too tight. Doesn't let go.

Body goes numb.

Can't do it. Can't let him hurt me. Can't let him kill me.

Nowhere to run. Nowhere to hide.

Let go.

Scream tears from my throat. Head raises off pillow. Whips to side. Slams into Braxton's face. Hard. Impact rattles my brain. Crack sounds. Cartilage snaps.

Braxton howls.

Crimson streams from nose. Pitches forward. Onto me.

Panic increases. Need him off. Need him away. Need to get free. To fight back.

Strain against bonds. Cuffs too strong. Won't give in. Straps are weaker. Thinner. Metal creaks. Bed frame slices. One frays.

"Riley, what the fuck?" Braxton yells. "Dude, you broke my fucking nose!"

Arm comes free. Under my command.

Wrap around his neck. Squeeze. Pull him closer.

He struggles. Gasps. Sputters. Tries to resist. To push me away.

Fear makes me strong.

Neck is close. Teeth find purchase. Rip through skin. Muscle. Scrape against bone.

Flesh is soft. Wet. Warm.

"Riley! Let go of me, you asshole! Fucking stop!"

Braxton fights back. Screams. Claws.

Blood sprays from wound. Covers my face. Braxton's face. My neck. My chest. My arm. Coats tongue.

Braxton collapses. Weight too much. Slips out of my grasp. Lands on floor in heap. Heavy hit. Loud thump.

Gasps for air. Slams hand to injury. Tries to slow bleeding. Too much escaping. Too fast for him to stop. Slides backward. Collides with door.

"Doctor!" he cries. "Doctor, help me. Open this fucking door!"

Pulls hand away from neck. Shines with blood. Neck squirts. Bangs on metal. Again. Again. Again. Leaves crimson streaks. Begs for help.

Door rips open. Braxton falls into hall. Onto Doctor's feet. Reaches for Andrew. Wraps fingers around ankle.

Doctor doesn't move. Mouth hangs open. Face pales. Shocked.

Andrew scrambles for Braxton. Drags him onto his feet. Covers wound. Tries to help.

"I told you this was a bad fucking idea," Andrew admonishes. Not horrified. Pissed. Livid. Not at Braxton. Thinks he's innocent. A victim. No, at me. At the madman. "Jesus, fuck. Get emergency down here before this guy bleeds out! He's missing a chunk of his goddamn neck. Do it, now!"

Doctor still frozen. Arms slack. Staring at me. At blood. At what I've done.

"I said now, Doctor Barrows! Do your fucking job!" Andrew turns away. Drags Braxton along beside him.

Braxton is dead weight. Makes it difficult. Limp legs. Loose grip. Stumbles along.

"Y… yes," Doctor whispers. Remembers himself. Hands flutter over jacket. Dig through pocket. Find phone. Dial numbers.

Follows Andrew. Braxton.

Leaves me all alone.

All alone.

Afraid. Drenched. Tied up.

Howling.

Footsteps recede. Voices fade. Intercom sparks to life.

"Code blue. Psychiatric unit. Code blue. Psychiatric unit. Code blue."

Message repeats on loop. Running sounds.

No one looks for me. No one cares. No one notices.

Abandon me. Leave me. Let me fall apart.

Overcome by fury.

I am nothing. I am no one.

Thrash against restraints. Tear at cuff on other arm. Dig fingers beneath the fabric.

Rip. Shred. Claw.

CHAPTER 23

THEN

AGAINST MY WILL, MY BODY FINDS RELEASE, CLIMAXING AND FILLING Allison's mouth to the brim. Moaning with pleasure, she sucks me dry. When the last ounce of my seed is spent, she tips her head back and grins.

Blood tints the tips of Allison's fangs. That snakelike tongue of hers darts across her mouth. She raises one finger to the corner, dabbing at the crease as though finishing a meal.

"You really are *so* sweet," she taunts, rising lithely from the floor on grossly elongated limbs. She's as tall as me now, stretched and gangly. The sight is sickening. "Full of sugar. I swear, you taste like fresh buttercream. It's been a long time since I've sampled such a good samaritan."

Splaying her palms across my chest, she leans in close, touching her forehead to my own. Her once smooth skin has aged inexplicably. Wrinkles carve deep grooves over her brow and around her eyes. Centimeters away, those piercing red orbs fix on me.

Though I know I should, I can't keep the disgust from my expression, a fact she clearly does not miss.

Allison's head tilts to the side as she studies my revulsion. The bones in her neck crack, shifting against each other. Her hair, previously so alluring, hangs in dull, limp sheets from her skull, brushing along my collarbone and making me shiver. Bare scalp, scabbed and rotting, appears in the thinner patches. The sites ooze putrid yellow pus which drips down toward her ears and dries in the creases.

She blinks slowly, drawing back disturbingly parched lips into a sneer. From deep within her throat, a vibration begins. Quiet at first, it steadily increases. Horror seizes me as she opens her maw impossibly wide. With a snap, her jaw unhinges.

Allison inhales a rattling breath through the dangling orifice. A faint glow emanates from my body, growing brighter as it forms into a dense stream of something gaseous. Abruptly, my skin starts to burn, set ablaze by an unseen force, and my heart stutters, threatening to halt completely. The substance draining from my form coalesces and curls like smoke, drifting toward her, trailing down her throat, and disappearing into the dark chasm.

As suddenly as it had appeared, the mist fades, taking with it the all-consuming heat. Allison collapses against me, trembling in ecstasy. Despite the warmth of her body, goosebumps erupt over my core and limbs. Hollowness settles into my chest, as well as a sense of gnawing unease, an awareness of something essential missing.

"Oh," she sighs. "Oh, Riley. That was incredible. I can't tell you how much I *needed* this." Her eyes roll back into her head, and her hands spasm. Allison's fingers curl into claws, and the points of her talons rip into my pecs, sinking farther and farther until her nails vanish.

Crying out in pain, I recoil from her grasp, retreating as much as the cross bearing me will allow. I thrash against my restraints, desperate to break away, but the bonds hold, and I can't free my extremities. Bucking and squirming, I attempt to shove her, to thrust her off of me, but all of my efforts fail.

"Sshtop!" I bellow, words blocked by the bit. "Aarraagh, fwuck!" I scream. "Guoffme," I plead repeatedly.

Gleefully, Allison squeezes, strengthening her grip. She looks up at me, lids heavy with satisfaction. One at a time, she withdraws her digits, plucking them out of my flesh, leaving me quaking in intolerable agony.

"What's wrong?" she taunts. Her monstrous face contorts into a mockery of pity. "Am I being too rough, Big Boy?" Shaking her head, she wipes her hands on her thighs, painting them with streaks of gore. "Just wait. I'm only getting started, Riley."

The acrid taste of fear coats my tongue as I strive to calm my harsh breathing.

Faster than humanly possible, Allison skirts behind the cross. Her footsteps are soundless, and once again I can't see what she's doing. My neck refuses to swivel enough. I barely have time to consider the dangers that await me before the wood pressing into my spine creaks.

Without warning, the structure tips back toward the floor, hurling me horizontal until I'm level with the ground, shocking my already reeling senses.

"I love this cross," Allison whispers into my ear. Her tone is deadly. "It looks simple enough, but I assure you, appearances *are* deceiving. It's one of my favorite toys. So useful. *Very* handy." She drags her thumb over my lower lip and blinks at me. "As long as I have you strung up across these beams, I can position you however I please. Do whatever I want, whenever I want. You're a fly in my web, Big Boy." She parrots my earlier thought. "Helpless. Trapped. Mine for the taking."

"Fwuck woo," I mutter, casting her a vicious glare.

"All in good time," she answers. "You're so much fun to play with, Riley, and my venom will keep you hard. Eager. Ready for me. I have so many plans."

Allison lowers her mouth to mine, forcing her vile tongue between the bit and my lips.

Out of instinct, my head rockets forward, slamming squarely into her face. The harsh impact rocks her stance and sends her staggering back several feet. Astonished, she raises her hand to her nose. When she pulls it away, it's coated with something black, tarlike and sticky.

Blood. But, it's not like mine. Not like the rivulets that drip from the punctures in my chest and run down onto the floor in puddles of merlot. The liquid sizzles as it comes into contact with the air, then flakes away as though carried by a breeze.

"That," she hisses through clenched teeth, "was unnecessary." She adjusts the broken cartilage, putting it back in place where it should be. "I thought you'd know better than to fuck with me."

Calmly, Allison reaches for the space below my ass and unlatches a small, attached plank from the cross beams. I hadn't known the board was hooked underneath. She takes her time, humming as she works, the sound at odds with the steadily growing apprehension enveloping me.

Confused, I watch as she swivels the plank away, stretching it off to one side. She moves in the opposite direction and unlatches another piece, repeating the same process in reverse. When she's satisfied, she locks them in place, then tests the strength of their hold, shaking them and leaning against them individually.

Allison doesn't say a word as she demonstrates their purpose. Using the boards for leverage, she hoists herself on top of me, deliberately straddling my waist. She rests her knees against the solid surfaces, adjusting her position until her pussy settles on the tip of my dick.

Starting at my collarbone, she touches me lightly, lovingly. She caresses the curves of my frame. Her fingertips dance over the dips of my hips. Then, her nails drag delicately back up my sides, bumping along the outcroppings of my ribs and slicing open the first few layers of skin.

Bracing myself, I shut my eyes, anticipating what must be coming.

She doesn't move. Just hums. Waits. Bores into me with that devilish stare of hers.

Cracking open my lids, I risk a glance at her face.

Allison smiles. Pauses. Seems to think about something humorous. A quiet chuckle escapes her lips.

"You've been a bad boy, Riley," she says. "You broke the rules. Now, there will be repercussions. It's time to play."

Before I can comprehend what she means, Allison splays her fingers across my sides. Her eyes darken, and her lips thin. One by one, she presses her talons into my flesh, burrowing deep.

Screaming through the gag, I watch in horror as her fingers disappear completely.

"How does it feel to have a woman inside of *you* for a change?" she taunts. "Is it everything you could ever wish for? Your darkest fantasy?"

Mirroring my movements from when I had her beneath me, she withdraws her digits. They slide out until they're almost free, then slam back in.

The room fills with my tortured screams.

She stops for a moment, considering me. "You're so wet for me, Riley." Blood drips down her wrist. Again and again, she fingers my ribs. "So tight. It's like you've never done this before, Big Boy. Am I your first? Did you save yourself for me?"

"Awishin," I plead, hoping to appeal to the woman I met at the bar. "Fwuck. Shtop. Don do dis. Aarraagh, no! No mwor. Pwease."

"I'm sorry, what was that? You want me to stop?" Allison asks.

I know better than to believe her words are sincere. She's set on malice and depravity. When she'd said I'd pay for my actions, she'd meant it with every fiber of her being.

What have I gotten myself into?

"Hmm, stop. Like your friend did at The Rabbit Hole when he preyed on the drunkest woman on the dancefloor? The one you let him lead away?"

Shit. Braxton? Am I supposed to pay for his sins?

"I saw everything. And, we are the company we keep."

Allison drives her fingers down to the hilt again. She swipes her finger across a nerve. Sharp anguish zips through my frame. "Oh, did you like that? It's hard to tell. With you all tied down, I don't get to feel you squirm the way you felt me."

My eyes roll back into my head as she repeats the movement, then scrapes her nails along the underside of my ribs.

"That's the spot," she coos. Leaning forward, she presses her lips to the space just below my ear. "Or, would you rather I find one of those tight little tendons? Pluck it like a fucking guitar string?"

"Awishin. Lemme gwo. Pwease," I beg through fractured mewls and whimpers. "Lemme gwo!"

"No? That's not your thing? Or, did I misunderstand? You're not communicating clearly. Maybe you should spit it out, huh? Or, just relax a bit. The first time can be a little painful. Want me to pull out? Try something different?"

Only then do I feel Allison's tail slithering up my leg. She angles its barbed tip to my exposed entrance, the unprotected space between my cheeks.

"I bet you want me to fill all of your holes. After all, I know that's what you wanted to do to me, isn't it? You naughty thing."

Thrusting her tail into the tight crevice, Allison buries the extra appendage inside of my ass, then sinks her teeth into the delicate flesh around my nipple. She keeps up a relentless pace, and I'm helpless as she punctures my lungs with her claws and shreds my internal organs to ribbons.

Unexpectedly, Allison ends her assault, then just as quickly, slashes out with her talons, attacking me once again. Blood sprays across her stomach and chest. The tips cut decisively through my flesh, rending skin from muscle and severing arteries.

Over and over, her nails slice across my body. Unable to breathe, I can do nothing but watch as her blonde hair stains pink. Splatter quickly obscures her features. Her breasts glisten with ruby splotches. Droplets fall from her peaked nipples. Her disgruntled roars echo through the bedroom, so loud they rupture my eardrums.

My body jerks. Curls into itself. Contracts in torment. Trembles in misery.

And when she finally stops, I'm certain this is it. The end. An escape from her clutches. Death offered in a gruesome package.

The end sounds surprisingly sweet.

A black haze creeps into my vision. My heart slows its rhythm, threatening to drag me into the abyss.

She licks the gore from her fingers and lowers down. Seats herself onto my blood-soaked shaft. Dips her tongue into the remnants of my stomach. Lets it settle into the gouges she's made.

To my horror, the wounds begin to stitch back together. Every last one of them. Everywhere she touches. Regrowing. Fading.

My vision clears, and my heart resumes its frantic pace.

"That was enjoyable, too," she admits as the last blemish disappears. Her eyes flash with hostility. "Was it good for you?" she taunts. "Would you like to do it again?"

I swallow, at a loss for words. Stay perfectly still. Try not to provoke her rage.

Allison begins to rock. Swivels her hips. Grinds against my body. Increases her speed until she reaches a steady rhythm.

I look away. Shut my eyes. Pretend this isn't happening. Ignore her completely.

"Ah, ah, ah," she admonishes. "I don't think so, Riley. I want you to watch. I want you to see it all. To feel it. To know you're mine, and there's no escape from my whims. Are you going to challenge me again?"

She cups my chin, tries to turn my head, to make me face her, but I resist.

Her movements slow, then halt completely. Her body becomes rigid. Solid marble. A statue.

Eventually, Allison shifts, and I dare to take one more glimpse at the monster who controls my fate. I know it's a fool's errand, but for just a second, I allow myself to hope beyond hope that she's changed her mind. That she's decided to release me. To end this torment because I no longer want to play her game.

But, she hasn't. Not even close. Everything in her expression, in her posture, says the exact opposite.

Instead, she holds something in her hands. She must have grabbed it from the table near the cross.

A metal object. Shining steel. A loop vaguely shaped like sunglasses with two half-moon structures curving at each of the ends.

Allison wraps the device around the back of my head and situates it across my temples. The fit is snug. Squeezes too tight. Unyielding. Unforgiving.

"Open wide," she instructs, angling the strange ends toward my face. For a moment, I think she means for me to open my mouth, but she tips the device in the opposite direction.

Toward my eyes.

Realization strikes. It's not for my mouth. Why would it be? She's already controlling that with the bit. This is something else.

I know what it is. I've seen it before. Not in person, but in movies. In horror films.

A speculum.

Shaking my head as hard as I can, I try and fail to escape her clutches.

It doesn't matter. Allison uses the crook of her arm to still my movements and easily slips the metal crescents under my lids. First, one eye. Then, the next. Holding back the thin folds. Forcing them to remain open. Not giving me the chance to blink. Or shut her out. To protect them.

"Give it up," she commands. "You made a bargain you didn't understand. You were warned, but you did it anyway. Choices have consequences. And, you know what?" she asks. "You're going to pay for yours."

Allison lets the tip of her talon hang above my lens. Not touching. But, only barely.

"No one even knows you're gone. Not one soul. Not one living creature. You won't be missed. Maybe eventually, but by then, it will be *far* too late."

Sobs rip from my chest. Drown out her words. Punctuated by my intermittent screams.

"Because from this moment on, you are no one, Riley Sylers. Nothing. Not a man. Not even a human. Just my little plaything."

CHAPTER 24

NOW

THE DOOR IS OPEN…

I remember.

CHAPTER 25

THEN

"ARE YOU HAVING A GOOD TIME, RILEY?"

Allison lowers her face. Knows the answer. Taunting me. Teasing.

Nuzzles space behind my ear. Sucks lobe between her lips. Snakelike tongue grazes the edge. Pinches it between razor-sharp teeth. Lets them sink in, piercing flesh.

"Because I must admit, you are exactly what the doctor ordered. Absolutely *delicious*."

Can't even groan. Too weak to reply. To fight. Mouth won't form words. Throat too tired. Raw. Thoughts too sporadic. Coming in pieces. Body disengaged from mind. Protecting me. Shielding me from her actions. Begging to survive.

Mind disagrees. Wants to let go. To give in. To let life end. To fade into comfortable nothingness.

Has to be better than this.

If I could close my eyes... shut her out... Maybe could pretend I'm not here. Not trapped on this cross. No fiend straddling my waist.

Somewhere else. Somewhere pleasant. On a vacation. Hot, sandy beaches. Warm breeze. Crashing waves and drink in hand.

But, I can't. Device still in place. Fixed beneath my lids. Burrowing into delicate spaces metal should never be. Won't even let me blink.

Tears stream down, staining my cheeks. Doing nothing to soothe my eyes. They burn like fire. Too long exposed to air.

Pressure builds in my head where blood pools. No support from cross's frame. Hangs back, limply, angled toward floor. Muscles can't keep it raised.

Difficult to swallow at this angle. Drool escapes from corners of lips.

Allison releases ear. Shifts upright. Plants her hands on my shoulders and tap... tap... taps my collar bone. Seeking acknowledgment. Makes her feel powerful. In control. Even a grunt. A groan. A whisper.

Don't respond. Provokes her to anger. Taps become torture. Tips dig into deltoids. Drag down. Tear through skin. Deep gouges follow their path. Stretch across pecs. Trail off to the side.

Pauses and waits. Sees if it makes a difference.

It doesn't. Focus on breathing. On sound of heartbeat throbbing in ears. On anything but her.

Allison palms my ribs. Her hands are warm. Contrast with chill that's overtaken me. Exposed to the air. Drained of essence. Nearing the end, I think.

She pouts. Sticks out lower lip. Tuts in disapproval and shakes head, watching me.

"Don't tell me you've decided to be boring." Rolls eyes. Shifts gaze to ceiling. "You don't even have a little whimper for me? A few hours ago, you were desperate for me to touch you, to be inside of me."

Hours no longer matter. Time is endless. Eternity in a second. Hell of my nightmares with no hope of escape.

Allison shifts down to my hips. Blows out a breath. "Such a disappointment. I won't stand for it." Lowers her pussy onto my dick.

Searing agony. Once was pleasure, ecstasy. Now, sandpaper. Chaffing and wearing me away. She grinds against me. Burying me deeper. Deeper. Deeper...

She won't stop. Never stops. Over and over, claims me again. One way or another. Wraps her serpent tongue around my shaft. Pumps me with her hands. Rides me until I shatter. Climaxes so strong, they're torture. Little deaths.

Fought until I couldn't. Until muscles gave in. Until nerves stopped relaying correct information. Accustomed to misery at her command.

Won't show her what she's doing. She likes it. My fear. My pain. Lavishes in it. Keeps me hard with her venom. Cooperative. Captive. Screams her satisfaction. Licks her lips like I'm a delectable dessert. Praises me for being "*so* good." Strokes my chest. My abs. My hips. My legs. Cups my balls. Pinches my nipples. Caresses ass. Probes with her tail. Fills forbidden parts. Leaves me trembling.

Each time, more smoke. Emptier. Fading.

Until she changes. Unpredictable like storms. Switches tactics on a dime. Veers from sensual to insane at drop of hat. Chokes. Unhinges her jaw, impossibly large. Buries her fangs in my meat. Mauls me. Consumes me. Strips away my flesh. Cracks my bones. Pops joints. Rends me into pieces.

Then, lets me heal. Does it again.

Only makes things worse to complain. So, I tolerate. Let her take me. Count the mistakes I made that led me here.

Let Braxton take me out. Should have stayed home. Wanted to be there. Shut the world out. Spend evening with my game. Comfortable on couch. Eat shitty pizza. Wallow in pity.

Sat at the bar. Accepted his challenge. Flirted with a demon. Played along with her game.

Let him leave. Take date. Abandon me at The Rabbit Hole. Pay for drinks I didn't need.

Swallowed her poison. Down the hatch without question. Again and again and again.

Trusted pretty face. Curvy frame. Gorgeous eyes. Pouty mouth. Squeezable hips.

Thought I was safe. So wrong.

Didn't listen to Chester. Told me to leave things be. Blew him off.

Followed my rabbit down the alley. Back here.

She even warned. Tried to scare me away. Dismissed it. Every caution. Every red flag.

She's evil. Vile. Made of sin. A wicked thing. Wicked little rabbit. Pied piper for the broken and maimed.

I knew better. Still, here I am. Paying for my blunders.

Paying only way I can.

With my soul.

"OH, YES…" SHE MOANS. ROLLS HER HIPS. BOUNCES ON MY COCK. TOSSES her head back and cums.

Collapses onto me. Tilts face up to mine. Opens vulgar mouth. Inhales.

Blue mist leaves body. Fainter than before. Lighter each time. Must be nearly empty. So depleted.

Feel its absence. The hole where it was. The pieces of me she's taken.

Swirls into her parted lips. Steals what little energy I had. More blackness crowds vision. Tempting, sweet abyss.

Ready to fall over edge. Down. Down. Down. The real rabbit hole. The final journey. The last hurdle I'll ever meet.

Allison shudders. Elated. Younger now. Wrinkles gone. More human. No more pus. Skin radiant with health. With my life. Everything I've ever been. Could have been. Will never be.

"Fuck, I could do this for eternity." Garnet eyes lock with mine. Heavy with lust. Saturated with need. Nearly glowing.

Her satisfaction dims. Euphoria fades to disappointment. Disgust. Then, anger.

Unfocus my vision. Look through her. At bed I longed for. At popcorn on ceiling. At neon lights, still blaring. Beyond to waking sky behind window pane.

"You're being rude again. Ungrateful. After all I've given you? Seriously? That's just plain rude."

Peels chest off abdomen. Leans back on haunches. Spreads fingers wide. Examines talons.

"Men would kill to be where you are, Riley Sylers. Have killed, in fact. For me. For a taste of the bliss that comes with my venom. And here you are, not appreciating the experience I've provided you with."

Huffs indignantly. Lifts herself off my dick. Face splits into horrifying grin. Twisted.

Trails point of talon up seam where testicles meet. Over my shaft. Unzips skin.

No way to contain it. Body reacts on instinct. Automatic response.

Jerk beneath her. Let out gasp. Scream.

Comes out harsh whisper. Barely audible. Struggle for air. Deflate and quake.

"There you are," she sings. Plants gentle kiss on my nose. Moves to my lips. Rips off bit. Forces mouth open. Gags me with tongue. Blocks all sources of oxygen. Lets me panic. Suffocating.

Dread ebbs. Accept this moment. Accept final seconds. Welcome them.

Allison withdraws. Chuckles. Full of glee. "I was starting to think you were dead already," she says with sigh. Wriggles fingers like maggots on stomach. Rolls neck.

Bites her bottom lip. Extends tongue. Licks claw clean. "Look alive, Big Boy. I'm not done with you yet."

Knock comes from door. Startles her. Allison whips head toward it.

Reprieve.

"What do you want?" she yells.

Sounds of unlocking. Knob twists. Door swings open.

Intruder stands at threshold. Features bored. Not at all surprised by sight before him. One hand in pocket. Other lets go of knob and falls to hip.

"The hell you aren't, Princess," he says. "Do you have any idea what time it is?"

Allison groans. Not in pleasure. In annoyance. Climbs down off my body. Stands in her nakedness. Fully on display.

Doesn't cover me, either. Just saunters across floor.

To him.

To Chester.

Raises up onto her toes. Reaches.

Doesn't flinch. Lets her do it. Allows her to bury blood-soaked fingers in hair and pull face to hers.

Her appearance shifts. Tail disappears. Retracts into bare flesh above ass. Horns sink into skull. Hidden in blonde hair. Limbs shorten.

Kisses him passionately. Drops her hold. Hands back to normal. No talons. Short nails.

Moves to window. Presses forehead to glass. Stares down at street. Tilts head up to sky.

"It can't be dawn already," she complains. Crosses arms over chest. Sulks.

So odd. New behavior. Nothing like hardass bartender I met.

"Time flies in Wonderland. You know that." Chester walks to bed. Grabs her shirt off floor. Tosses it to her.

Easily catches it. Slips it over head. Conceals her breasts.

"You're a spoilsport." Voice indignant.

"This is what you pay me for, Allison. To keep you alive."

"No, I pay you to take care of my needs." Plops down on mattress. Flexes ankles.

"That's the same goddamn thing." Retrieves her pants. Passes them into outstretched hand. "Don't fight me. It's time to kill this asshole. Rip out his heart and hunker down until dusk."

"I'm still hungry," she answers. Slips one leg into bottoms. Then, the next.

"And, I don't care. Remember what happened last time?"

"Come on." Stands to button them. "Are you going to hold that against me forever?" she gripes. "It was centuries ago."

"Decades ago," Chester corrects. "People have cameras in their phones now. Social media. Next time you catch fire because you misbehaved and find yourself running bare-ass naked through the streets, someone's gonna film that shit. They'll expose you and all of your sisters. I won't be able to protect any of you then."

"Fucking humans," she snaps. "They can't leave well enough alone. None of them. I swear, they ruin everything."

"I can't argue with that," Chester replies. "Now, are you going to take care of this, or do I have to?"

"Fine," Allison relents. Steps away from window. Crosses space back to me. "You know, I didn't always have to hide like this. People used to send us offerings! Until the Church threw a fit." Sighs. "I miss the old days." Trails fingertips from my toes to calves, to thighs, to stomach, to chest. "You're right, though. You're always right. I hate it."

"And yet, you never listen, do you?" Moves to join her. Stands by other side of body. Doesn't touch, but scoffs at sight.

Breathy laugh. Allison tucks hair behind ear. "What fun would that be?"

"The kind of fun that means I don't have to cover for you constantly. Or dispatch civilians who happen to see you when they walk past your lair. Or bury you and tend to your wounds while you recover. Sounds like great fun to me. Just grand."

"That's because you don't know how to have a good time." Allison considers me. Brushes a section of hair off my forehead. Almost lovingly. Makes me recoil. Tremble. "Can't I keep this one, Chester? Just this once? He still has some life in him. I want to play with him again. He could be my pet…"

Chester rolls eyes. Reaches for cuff binding wrist. "That's not how it works, Princess."

"I know," Allison admits. Stops Chester from undoing latch. "Just… give me a minute. There's one more thing I need."

"Not this again," he complains.

Allison dismisses.

Chester crosses room. Grabs bench under window. Drags it over to me. Sits down. Leans elbows on knees and waits. "You're gonna let him live, aren't you?"

"Mhmm," she answers. "This one is different. I like him." Blinks sweetly at me. Runs back of hand along jaw to my chin. "He's good. I can't help but think he would find his way back to me if I set him free. Do you think he might?"

"Maybe," Chester answers. Begrudging. "But, why would you want him to? You fucked him up, Allison."

"I did." Face full of pride. "I promised I would. He wanted it. Seriously, he begged to be used and tossed out. And, the sex… It was *divine*."

"They always want you. The sex is always good. Don't act like you're surprised. You're a goddamn succubus. It's what you do."

Allison places other hand behind my head. Lifts me so I'm level. Presses down on mandible under lower lip.

Mouth opens. Defenseless.

Lowers her lips to mine. Tongue not human yet. Still serpent. Long. Thin.

Trails across my palette until reaches soft spot near tonsils. Searches. Then, angles upward. Tip hardens to solid-steel.

Instant torment. Slices through flesh. Burrows up, up, up. Cuts through sinuses. Snakes into brain.

Suddenly stills.

Squirming sensation, then slow retreat. Back through tunnel she made. Into mouth. Slips away from me.

Iron coats cheeks. Lips. Thick. Heady.

Allison straightens. Doesn't retract tongue. Glistens with blood. Clutches something tiny. Little oval. No larger than pea. A pearl.

She blinks at me, then pulls it inside. Swallows the gland. Moans and grins.

"You're a part of me now, Riley Sylers," she says. Caresses my face. Tilts head. "I don't have to worry whether or not you'll come back to Wonderland. No matter where you go or how fast you run, I'll always be able to find you."

Watch in horror. Unable to speak.

"You're mine," she whispers into ear. "My personal toy, and I'm not done playing. Rest. Heal. I'll come for you when I'm ready."

"Great," Chester interrupts. "What am I supposed to do with him, huh? He can't stay here. They'll kill his stupid ass."

"Take him to the hospital," she commands. "He'll be safe there."

Irritated, Chester stands. Shoves away bench. Watches Allison as she leaves.

She stops. Turns back to me. Adds one more thing. "Don't you worry. This will all be over soon. You won't remember a thing. Well, not enough to matter, Big Boy."

Doesn't shut door. Unafraid. Leaves bedroom open.

Chester stands behind my head. Undoes restraints on my wrists. Clatter to floor with solid thunk. Studies my reaction.

Remain calm. Dazed. Stay still. Wait.

Chester smiles. Too large for face. All teeth. In wrong place. Upside down. So strange.

Removes device. Finally able to blink.

"She lied, you know," he says. "Nowhere is safe. Not from her. She should have killed you, you poor bastard."

Yes, all I can think.

CHAPTER 26
THEN

"Jesus, you're fucking heavy," Chester grumbles. "You look like a string bean. What are you? One-eighty? Not even two hundred pounds, I'd bet." Strong hands adjust my body. Fling me farther over his shoulder. Grip my hips. Waist near chin. Dangle down his backside. "But, you're all dead weight. Every last one of you. That's the problem. It always is." Grunts. Sighs. "She couldn't have left you with enough soul to walk down the stairs?"

Heavy footfalls. Every step is agony. Neck won't work. Too tired to bear weight. Leaves head suspended. Bounces against Chester's back. Steady rhythm rattles brain.

Throbbing between eyes. Behind nose. Somewhere deep. Intense. Aching.

Skull is too small. Brain too big. Feel it swelling. Filling every nook. Every cranny. Crushing against bone. Too much pressure. Worse than hangover. Ten times. Twenty. Fifty.

Blink. Try to ignore sensation. Clear my vision.

Apartment is dark. Not like before. Lit faintly by dawn. See patches on floor. Muted pink rectangles. Interrupt the shadows. Light. Then, gray. Then, light again.

How? From where? No windows. Only walls. Only stairs.

Turn gaze up to ceiling. *There.* Comes from above. Hadn't noticed last time. Too focused on her. On destination. Missed skylights overhead.

Must be top floor. Impossibly high. Everything else beneath.

Round and round. Staircase curves. Down. Down. Down. We descend. Leaving Wonderland. Leaving her. The life I had.

She took it. Ruined it. Destroyed it.

Destroyed me.

Chester trots easily. Never misses step. Doesn't bother with railing. Holds me tight to him.

"Of course not," Chester gripes. "She doesn't have to haul your zombie-ass out with the trash, so she couldn't care less. It's not her problem. One of these days, I won't be around to clean up her mess. What's she gonna do then?"

Doesn't want me to answer. Talking to himself. To the air.

Couldn't speak if I tried. Throat raw from screaming. Lungs struggle to expand.

Ears ring at slightest sound. Jaw tense from bit. Tongue nearly severed. Searing pain in sides.

Still feel her teeth. Chewing. Ripping. Feel her fingers. Puncturing skin. Digging through muscle. Wriggling. Rearranging. Scraping.

Bury it. Ignore it. Drive it out. Let it go.

Don't want to remember. None of it. Where I've been. How I got here. Who I am. What she did…

Wounds are closing. Slowly healing. Just like before. Stitching together. Mending. Disappearing.

No proof. No evidence. No one will know. No one will listen.

Except for bruises. Staying. Around wrists. Ankles.

Natural. Not supernatural. Not mending.

Nerves buzz. Relay information. Brain can't comprehend. Translates wrong.

Now come insects. Wasps. Caterpillars. Centipedes. Maggots. Crawling. Stinging. Burrowing. Biting. Squirming.

Not there. Not there. Not there.

Can't make it stop. Sensation overwhelming. Too much to process. To shut out.

No more stairs.

Chester slows. Winds down long hall. Door after door after door after door.

Not all closed. Used to be. Remember that.

No. Some open. Reveal obscure rooms. Blocked by figures. Hidden in gloom. Leaning in frames.

Chester watches. Doesn't flinch. Not afraid.

"Forget it. I'm not hauling your scraps out, ladies." Hard edge to Chester's voice. Assertive. "Do it your damn selves. I don't work for you."

Passes another room. Figure displeased. Hisses.

Gangly limb swipes at Chester. Incredibly fast. Claws graze shirt. Snag on fabric. Withdraw without damage.

Chester pissed. Swats her arm. Knocks her off balance.

"I like this shirt," he adds. "And, I'm not replacing it. Keep your talons to yourself."

Turns to face her. Silently dares her to move. To swipe again.

She doesn't. Stays out of reach. Shuts door. Locks self inside.

"Anyone else want to fuck with me today?" he asks.

Silence answers.

Journey resumes. Entrance close. In sight.

Chester halts. Repositions me. Frees one hand. Reaches two fingers into front pocket. Rummages. Digs out key.

Same one she had. Dangles from ring. Attached to rabbit's foot. Fluffy. White. Stained now at tip. Reddened fingerprints.

"You're one unlucky bastard, kid. But, you can be thankful she didn't feed you to them." Door swings open. Chester steps out of apartment. Pulls it closed behind him. "Allison's a wicked one, but the others have no restraint. You'd be dead already, and the way they do it makes even me sick." Slides key into lock. Twists knob, checking.

Dead. Would be easier. Would be painless. Would be mercy.

No more fear. No more creatures. No more existing.

But, not dead. Won't give in. Give her satisfaction.

Can't do that. Can't give up.

Need to get away. From here. From her. From him.

Escape.

Adrenaline pumps in veins. Energy fading. Fast. Completely drained. Spent.

Will body to cooperate. To stay awake. Protect itself. Survive this.

Doesn't listen.

Eyelids droop. Threaten to close.

Must keep watching. Must be aware. Must be ready.

Too much effort.

Fade before we reach next landing.

CHAPTER 27

NOW

FINGERNAILS CHIP. RESIST EFFORTS.

Keep clawing anyway. They snag and bleed. Catch on threads.

Nails separate from beds. Rip off. Take skin with them. Make bloody mess.

Doesn't stop me. Fear stronger than pain. No time to waste.

Move from one limb to next. Wrists. Ankles. Ignore cuffs. Focus on straps. Weak points. Thinner. Easier.

Pull them taught. Apply more pressure. Rub against metal frame. Use for leverage.

Hands go numb. Feet, too. No circulation. Turn purple. Blue.

Watch straps unravel. Splintering. Shredding. Fraying. Bit by bit.

Everything marred by stains. Red splotches. Dark fingerprints. Painted by my touch.

Like the rabbit's foot. The keychain. The one she had. Dyed by same thing.

Repress thought. Isn't helping. Can't let myself drift.

Stay in the moment. The present. See this through. Sever my chains.

Labor quickly. One arm free. One leg.

Last strap breaks. Falls limply to floor. Wraps around support. Disappears under bed.

It's done. No more restraints.

Color fades from extremities. Flex hands. Stretch legs. Roll ankles. Bend knees.

Everything responds. Too slowly, but does what I ask. Still weak. Shaky.

Twist around. Lower feet to tile. Touch laminate. Cold soaks in.

Must test strength. *Can I stand?* Maybe. Out of practice.

Lean forward. Hold tight to mattress. Add weight to soles. Carefully. Steadily.

Thighs tremble. Calves cramp. Warn me of fatigue. Of disuse.

Manage to pull self up. Straighten. Let go of bed. Barely.

Balance off. Wobbly gait. Head for wall. Use for support.

Travel around room. Movement awkward. Toes drag. Knees try to buckle.

Make it to corner. Out of sight of hall. From them. Anyone who may be waiting.

Heart pounds in ears. Rapid beat. Throbbing rhythm.

Try to breathe. To calm. To quiet.

Find control. Just a little. Enough to venture closer. Creep toward exit.

Can't see from here. Hallway behind me. Can hear, though. Close eyes. Listen intently.

For voices. For footsteps. For people.

Doctor Barrows. Andrew. Braxton.

No one there.

Might come back. Realize their mistake.

Can't have that.

Time passes. Not sure how much. Could be seconds. Could be minutes.

Adrenaline surges. Chokes me. Makes me quiver. Feel faint. Dizzy.

Realization hits.

Out of bonds. Now what? Can't stay.

Don't want to get caught. Need to get out. To get away. From here. From them. From her. From him. From…

Everyone.

Find someplace safe. Somewhere safe.

But, where?

Nowhere is safe. He said so. She'll find me. Track me. Hunt me down. Do it again.

The Queen of Hearts. No. Queen of Nightmares. Wicked little rabbit. Evil. Deadly.

But, she lies.

Have to believe that. Have to hope. Pray it wasn't true. That I can escape.

Finally, have a chance. Door is right there. Inches away.

Now's the time. Do something or be stuck. Locked away. Forgotten. Abandoned.

Swallow hard. Hesitate. Throat dry. Bile rising.

Force self to door. Peer around frame. Hall is empty.

Make decision.

Steel spine. Clench hands into fists. Step outside.

Go now. Do it quietly. Do it quick. Get out before they see me. Realize I'm not in cell. Not cuffed to bed.

Which way?

Press back to wall. Feels safer. No surprises. No sneaks.

Make self small. Choose a direction. Head for corner at end.

Hallway is long. Vision wavers. Shifts this way and that.

Feels familiar. Unsettling. Reminds me of apartment. Where she lives. Where she hunts. Where she waits. The trap she'd laid.

Not there, remind self. *Can't be there.* Hallway is bright. Clinical. Sterile. Lit by huge fluorescent panels.

No skylights overhead. No shadowy figures. No slashing claws.

Shove unease away. Not helpful. Only makes me anxious. Must focus on this. On task. On present.

Stop at the end. Hallway splits. Corners to the right and left.

Sign in the center. Screwed to wall. So many words. Numbers.

Try to read. To make sense of them. Eyes play tricks. Letters rearrange. Scramble into gibberish.

Defeat sinks in. Can't do this. Not alone.

Head falls. Slide down wall. Crumple onto floor. Feel it coming. A scream. Disaster.

Breath catches. Idea strikes.

Arrow on floor. Pointing. Leading.

To exit? To outside? To freedom? Survival.

Maybe not... Could be wrong. Go somewhere different. Cost me every-thing. Land me back in room. A prisoner.

Maybe, yes. Worth the risk?

Whatever it takes. Won't give up yet.

Drag self up. Stumble along with them. Let them guide. Rush down new path.

Bare feet slap on laminate. Too loud. Distracting. Sure to draw attention.

Can't hide the noise. Would mean going slower. Running out of time.

Stomach sinks.

New sound now. Low murmurs. Voices in distance. Still quiet. Getting louder. Coming from ahead.

Staff? Patients? Both?

Can't turn back. Have to hide. Avoid being seen.

Where?

Only option another room. One a few feet away. But, what if locked? Don't have key. Not a doctor. Not a nurse. *What then?* Won't be able to get in.

Closer. Closer.

They're coming.

Steady resolve. Move to door. Reach for handle. Press down on latch.

Click.

Swings open.

Inside, room dark. Not like mine. No patient. No one to scream. Alert them of presence.

Slip into shadows. Slink behind door. Draw it closed. Not all the way. Leave crack. A sliver. A way out. A way to keep track.

No motion sensors activate. No automatic lights. Lucky break.

Hold breath. Be quiet as mouse. Peer through gap. Scan outside.

There. Four doors away.

Walking. Not running. Talking. Not screaming. Casual exchange. Easy banter. Colleagues.

Hospital staff.

Unbothered. Must not know. Not be searching. Not interested in me. Not yet.

Pass by room. Don't spare glances. Notice anything.

Voices fade. Down the way I came.

Heading toward my room. My cell. The open door. The torn restraints. The bloody bed.

Might not know yet. Will definitely know soon. Can't be here then.

Clock is ticking. Getting late.

"Isn't it time we went to bed?"

My voice this time. Not hers. Slurred. Innocent. Naive.

Big mistake. Worst I ever made.

Shake head. Clear thought away.

Abandon room. Shut door behind me. Force legs to move. To carry me forward. Follow. Arrow after arrow.

Faster. Faster.

This way. That way. Duck under half-walls. Avoid nurses. Sneak around corners. Creep down stairs.

Single motive.

Get away. Have to get away. To get out. To keep going.

Don't look back.

CHAPTER 28

THEN

Shrieking metal hinges. Fresh air blasts face.

Consciousness returns. Resurfacing in haze. Dragging me from oblivion.

To reality. To pain. To fear.

No more shadows. No shield from rising sun. Soft pink of sunrise gone. Growing stronger every second. Vibrant orange.

Stings my eyes. Makes me wince.

Too long inside. In the dark. Place of nightmares. Wonderland.

Too long with her. The vixen. The demon. Soul devourer.

Succubus whore.

No more. Allison is gone.

No, not gone. Only away. Not with me. Not right now.

Soon, though. She promised. Said she'd find me. Use me again. Take what remains. Finish me off.

Eyelids like sponges. Don't block enough. Light soaks in. Slips passed crevices. Stabs into pupils. Lances through skull. Blinding. Searing. Stabbing into brain.

Headache pulses. Intense. Awful.

Tears rise. Make me blink. Blur vision enough to confuse. To disorient.

Fight them back. Struggle to clear sight. To make sense of surroundings.

Outside now. Still being carried. Still draped over Chester's shoulder.

Force neck to obey. To lift head. To study location.

Whispers of recognition. A path I walked. In the night. Hand in hers. Creature leading me to doom.

Recognize high rises. Loom over street. Over cracked concrete. Dirty asphalt.

No numbers on buildings. Just busted brick. Could be anywhere. Any city on Earth.

No pedestrians. All safe at home. Sleeping away the hours. Heedless of horrors in their midst. Dreaming of peaceful things. Too early to care. To rise from their beds. Just past sunrise.

No traffic, either. No cars or buses. No motorcycles or trucks. Street is silent. No rumbling engines. Backfiring tailpipes. Honking horns.

Stomach sinks. No one to help. To call for.

No saviors here.

Struck by sadness. Defeat. Loneliness. Heartbreaking ache. Regret. Complete and total.

Latches on to soul. The shreds left of it. Tattered pieces. Clings to hollow place in chest. Gaping void. Fills me with sorrow.

She's right.

She stole it. My life. All I had. Took pieces of me. One at a time. Drained me of memories. Siphoned everything unique. All the interesting parts. Enjoyable.

My essence is missing. Days are numbered.

Not myself. Not me.

Not anymore.

I am no one. No one. A broken man. Something inhuman. Devoid of chance. Opportunities stolen.

Not Riley. Riley gone. Dead at her hands. Soon to be erased.

Forget that name. Leave it behind. Old life over. Let last pieces of him go.

Quiet settles over me. Heavy like lead. Become empty. What she wants.

Only thing I can do. Choose to accept. To own. To adapt. To exist like this. Never to be whole.

A wraith. Empty vessel. Walking corpse.

Chester unconcerned. Moves fast. Heads for street. Stoops down. Lets go of one hip. Grabs onto something lower.

Another squeak. More hinges. This time to vehicle. Parked by side of road.

"You better not hurl in my car," he demands. Echo of similar command. Can't remember when. Where. Pulls door open. "I just had it detailed after the last idiot. Allison's exploits are getting expensive."

Sudden shift. Tipped backward off shoulder. Stuffed into backseat. Dumped onto cracked leather.

Car door slams. Loud boom. An explosion.

Frightens me. Sends me flying. Scooting across seat. Backing away from him. Scrambling for opposite side. Clawing for handle.

No handle there. Removed. Ripped off. Jagged hole where it belongs.

Fumble for lock. Car is old. Should be pin below window. Could pry it up. Loose.

Not there, either. Long gone.

Trapped inside. Like animal. Like prisoner. Nowhere to go. No hope to run.

Crumple and sob. Hoarse screams rip through throat. Fill up cab. Bounce back from every direction.

Chester raps knuckles on glass. Still on other side. Back to the building. Sneering at me.

"Knock it off, asshole," he barks. "Don't draw attention to yourself. If you do, you'll have hell to pay. Got it?"

Got it?

Attention? From who? From nonexistent strangers? Some imaginary hero?

Swipe tears off cheeks with wrist. Slide down slowly. Onto side. Stifle cries. Stare at ceiling. Bite tongue.

Chester steps back. Turns away from window. Leans body against car. Casual. Calm.

Another voice sounds. Speaks to captor. Cool and detached. Female. Not far away.

Who? Sounds familiar. Vaguely. A memory at the edge of thoughts.

Sniff. Wipe snot on arm. Haul self up. Use front seat for support. Peer outside. Find her.

There. Standing next to building. One we came out of. Only feet away.

A brunette. Looks rough. Dark circles under eyes. Tangled hair. Pale skin. Makeup smudged. Rumpled club clothes.

Fragment of recognition. Stumbling under flashing lights. Sloshing cup. Man with arm around her.

Search for name. *Know it?* Knew it. Certain of that.

Mouth tries to form words. "D... Dy..."

Nothing else comes.

Lean forehead against glass. Close eyes. Shut out sun.

They speak. Sounds distorted. Hard to make out. Muffled by barrier and space.

Decide to watch. Try to read lips.

Squint at mouths. Focus hard.

Chester beside her now. Must have left when not looking. Stands close. Seem acquainted.

"...let him go?" she asks. Gestures at car. At me. "Why did you..."

Chester shakes head. "...tried to talk her out... stubborn pain in my ass. You know what she's... dispose of a body... drive the fucker downtown and..."

Woman laughs. Rolls eyes. Reaches into pocket. Pulls out cigarettes. Lights one. Lifts to her mouth.

Flame sparks. Ignites. Gray smoke curls. Up. Up. Up.

Like soul. What was stolen from me.

She sucks in fumes. Blows into Chester's face.

He swats air. Grumbles. Flips her off.

"...dangerous. She knows better than..." woman continues. Grabs another cigarette. Lights with hers. Hands to Chester. "...sisters find out..."

Takes a drag. "Yeah, well." Shrugs his shoulders. Makes hand sign for money. "...pays the bills, Dynah, and... needs me. So do you. Those bitches in there would eat you for... let them. You better... and lock this place down before one of them gets..."

Woman named Dynah finishes smoke. Drops it to sidewalk. Crushes under shoe. Straightens up. "That's a you problem. I'm not the one... chases them down and shit. You're their guardian, Kaibyo, so drag the dumbass away and... Do your damn job."

"Just like your mother," he complains. "Just like Allison. Always..."

"Screw you." Shoves his shoulder. Playful. Not mad. "... get back upstairs to the friend... made sure he was distracted so she could... still passed out. He won't be a problem."

"Make sure he isn't." Chester finishes cigarette. Grinds it like she did. Walks backward. Takes several steps toward car. "Neither of us needs anyone to connect the dots."

Woman named Dynah nods. Waves at Chester. Opens building door and steps inside.

Chester rounds hood. Slides into driver's seat. Buckles seatbelt. Turns key in ignition. Throws into drive. Pulls out onto road.

"I know you were watching us, asshole. If you're smart," he says. Looks at me in rearview mirror. "You'll forget everything you saw and heard. Are you smart? Huh? Or am I going to have to shoot you before I can drop you off? She'd be so damn disappointed, but I wouldn't."

Tilts head toward front passenger seat. Pops open glove box. Full of papers. Junk. On top, gun in holster.

Strokes it with thumb.

Smart? Forget? Am I?

Swallow hard. Try to shrink. Make self small.

"That's a good boy," Chester praises. Clicks box shut. "You were never here. You don't know me. You don't know her. You don't know where the fuck you were or how you got there. Understand?"

Lean face against window. Let cold seep into skin. Stare at passing city. At sun overhead. At street after street after street.

Breath makes glass fog. Obscures journey.

Forget. Forget it all. Forget, and live.

Maybe that's enough?

Will never be enough. Nothing will. Not anymore.

CHAPTER 29

THEN

Hospital isn't far.

Chester drives around back. Doesn't go into structure. Where visitors would be. People who might ask questions. Notice something wrong.

Pulls into employee lot instead. Many vehicles. All empty.

No other drivers. No one to witness the drop.

Parks close to building. Not in marked space. Butted up against wall. Tight gap. Smart move. That side won't open now. No room for doors to swing.

Turns off engine. Rumble dies. Song on radio cuts out. Chester stops humming.

Silence. Only sounds of our breathing.

Chester sits back. Head hits the rest. Closes lids for a minute. Opens again. Stares into rearview mirror.

Haven't moved. Still pressed against window. Studying him. Trying to predict. To protect.

Moments pass. Stays there. Keeps hands on wheel. Firm grip.

Decides waited long enough. Lets out grunt. Snatches his keys. Shoves them into pocket. Pushes front door open. Steps out and walks to back.

Wish to disappear. Vanish into thin air. Pull off impossible escape. Stay out of his reach.

Do best I can. Slip down to floor. Curl up between front and back seats.

Door across from me opens. Same squeaky hinges. Makes me shudder.

Chester bends down. Arms on roof. Props weight against them. Fills up exit with body. Leans toward me. Torso in car. Head cocked off to side.

"Let's go, man. I don't have all day." Sounds tired. Little resentful. Like he doesn't want to be here, either. Wants to get this over with.

Not ready. Don't know what happens next. Funny feeling.

Not just fear. Dread. A deep intuition. Can't ignore it.

Stay still. Don't make move. Lock up. Hold breath. Wait to see.

Chester sighs. Lets head hang. Shakes it. "Hiding over there isn't going to save you. One way or another, you're getting out of my car. So, you can either crawl your ass over here or I can drag you out. Don't make this more difficult than it has to be."

Face hard as stone. Drums fingers on top of vehicle. Tiny booms echo through cab.

"No," I whisper. So quiet. Comes out gritty. Attempt to be brave. "Staying here."

"He speaks…" Chester raises eyebrows. Wrinkles spread across forehead. Seems surprised. Laughs. "Thought the cat might have gotten your tongue." Blinks. Scoffs. Opens eyes again. Vivid green irises. Pupils narrow slits. "Guess not. See, that's my job, and it can certainly be arranged. So, are you going to behave, or am I going to have to make you listen?"

Swallow hard. Breathe in. Hold. Blow out. "No," I repeat.

"Fucking figures." Rolls eyes. Glares at me. Nostrils flare. "You little bastards never learn."

Chester moves fast. Shouldn't be possible. Releases ceiling. Bends. Reaches for feet.

Already pulled close to me. No room to move out of way. Latches onto ankles easily.

Kick out. Fight hold. Roll onto stomach. Twist. Squirm. Hang on to base of passenger seat.

Flips me over. Squeezes harder. Bruising. Cutting off circulation.

Strive to remove fingers. Break grip.

Swats hands away.

Laughs again. Low vibration. Almost a purr. Sound resonates deep. Coming from chest.

Shock takes me. Stare in horror. Watch fingernails sharpen. Long, white tips.

Snag on fabric of jeans.

Shred cuffs. Slice into skin. Leave trails of glistening red.

Cry out. Covers mouth with hand. One quick tug with other. Hauls me across floor like bag of sand.

Back bumps over raised center. Pops spine like rice treats. Carpet grates. Sands skin beneath shirt. Trim crushes hips. Ribs. Shoulder blades.

Slam onto asphalt. Ground beside car. Skull bounces on impact. Snaps up and falls back. Teeth smack together. Something cracks.

"See?" he asks. Barely out of breath. "Wouldn't it have been better if you'd just done what I asked?" Drops my legs. Wipes hands on pants. Grimaces in disgust. "Now, I'm all filthy. Blood stains, you know. Jesus, I hate doing this shit."

Was already dirty. Where she touched. Tainted. Painted crimson by blood-drenched fingers. Hair. Face.

Head lolls to side. Hard to pay attention. Too dizzy. Too much pain. World spinning too fast. Feel sick.

Chester doesn't care. Busy searching my pockets. Digging out phone. Wallet. Keys.

Tosses them back into car. Bangs door shut. Looks at me with disinterest.

"This is how it's gonna work. When I leave, you're gonna go right up to the front door of this damn hospital and tell them you've been mugged. Got it?"

Mugged? Not mugged. Drugged.

Kidnapped. Tortured. Raped.

"And, I'm gonna make sure it's convincing."

Chester's face changes. Cruel. Menacing.

Roll onto side. Use forearms to inch toward front of vehicle. Drag body slowly. Over potholes. Broken glass. Rock chips.

Not fast enough.

Booted foot crashes into back. Knocks air out of me. Lungs seize.

Panic rises. Scramble to get away.

Several more punts. Hard hits. One to head. One to stomach. One to legs.

Curl up. Protect core. Gasp. Choke on fluid. Hot. Iron and salt. Dribbles from lips.

Finally, stops. Cleans shoe on my jeans.

Crouches again. Low voice. Deadly.

Forces me to look. Traps me with gaze. Green eyes swirl. Hypnotizing. Convincing.

"Keep your fucking mouth shut. She knows where to find you, which means *I* know where to find you. And, if I have to come back here to make you see things my way, you'll have hell to pay, just like I said."

Spits on ground beside me. Recoil. Whimper.

Man stands. Steps over my frame. Opens door and slides into driver's seat.

Engine rumbles to life. Car shifts into gear. Window rolls down. He leans out. Smiles at me.

"You were mugged. That's exactly what happened. And if you tell the truth, they won't believe you anyway. They'll think you've lost your shit. So, it's your move, asshole."

Rolls up window. Drives away.

CHAPTER 30

THEN

Sky turning gray. Cloudy. Foreboding.

In parking lot. Behind big building. Bleeding.

Why? Where? Don't remember coming here.

Body screaming in agony.

Lie still for a while. Draw in shaky breaths. Chest burns. Joints ache. Every movement torturous.

No one comes. Finds me. Offers help.

All alone.

Dying?

So afraid.

Not ready. Won't give in.

Roll carefully onto stomach. Don't think about grinding in sides. Popping in wrists.

Face falls into dirt. Dust chokes me. Makes me cough. Cuts off airway.

Extend arms. One at a time. Stretch out over head. Slam palms into asphalt.

Dig fingers into cracks. Make handholds. Grit teeth. Power through body's complaints.

Pull. With everything I have. Drag. Inch by inch. Excruciating effort. Takes a lifetime.

"H..." Lips won't form words. Tongue dry. Sticks to roof of mouth. "Help." So weak. "Help... Help me..."

Fingers find building. Corner nearby. Continue clawing until I reach it.

Hold on to it. Use for leverage. Haul self carefully onto knees. Lean against concrete. Find courage to keep going.

Overhead, clouds release. Heavy rain pounds earth.

Body trembles. Shakes. Wants to collapse. Quit.

Won't let it. Force one foot beneath me. Then, the next. Use last bit of strength to stand.

Thunder booms. Lightning streaks across sky. Wall grows damp. Slippery.

Scream. Vent frustration and misery. Pour out of my core like oil. Like poison, consuming me.

Step. Step. Make self walk.

Ankles wobble. Lose balance. Nearly trip me.

Feet drag as I go. Leave bloody trails. Droplets of ruby splatter pavement. Wash away in seconds. No trace.

Down an alley. Past dumpsters. Splash through muddy puddles. Soak shoes. Squish wetly beneath me.

Alley ends. Opens to street. City traffic. Busy.

Cars pass. Honking. Ignoring. Spraying muck everywhere.

Go where?

Road to left. Heads off through skyscrapers. Don't know where it leads. Long journey. No time.

Must find refuge. People who care.

Loop to right. Path much simpler. Clear destination. Butts up to entrance of building. Sliding glass doors. Large awning overhead. Vehicle out front. Ambulance waiting.

Ambulance.

Hospital.

Salvation.

Figures talking next to it. Wearing uniforms.

Paramedics.

Don't see me. Too busy. Caught up in conversation.

Make decision. Compelled.

Go right. Go to them.

Lurch forward. Past benches. Raised planters. Small trees.

Almost there. So close. A few more feet. Can taste it. End is near.

Don't know how, but keep going. Driven by fear. Adrenaline. Urgency.

Not paying enough attention. Too focused on goal. Trip over curb. Stumble. Fall forward. Land harshly on hands and knees.

"Help..." I grind out. "Please..."

One man turns. Finally sees. Mouth falls open. Eyes widen in shock. Horrified. Freezes.

Other notices change. Follows first's gaze. Discovers disturbance.

Me. Busted and helpless.

First one takes off. Ignores rain. Abandons second. Feet pound on sidewalk. So quick. Skids to halt by me. Sends debris flying.

Calls for the second. Drops down to my side. Clutches my shoulder. Rolls me onto back. Searches my body. Surveys injuries.

"Sir," he says. Voice calmer than behavior. "What's happened? Do you need assistance?"

Can't speak. Can't answer question. Too exhausted. Hard to think. Giving up completely.

"Get a doctor, now!" he orders partner. "I'll try to stabilize him, but I need a gurney and assistance. Stat!"

"On it!" Other man dashes away. Fast footsteps head toward building. Sliding door whooshes. Opens. Hear his voice inside. Calling for aid.

"Everything's going to be okay, sir. I don't know what happened to you, but you've made it to the hospital. You're safe here."

Safe? No. Not safe. *Nowhere is safe.*

Don't know why, but know *that*. Feel it in every part of me.

Laughter erupts from throat. Quiet at first. Then, hysterical.

Violent. Brittle. Angry.

Man looks confused. A little frightened. Lips thin. Face sours. Turns strange.

"Save your strength," he urges. "We'll get you squared away. That's what we do here, okay? The doctors are coming."

Coming?

Coming.

So is she.

CHAPTER 31

NOW

"RILEY..."

Voice in head. Not mine. Hers. Singsong tone. Sweet like poison. Calling to me. Beckoning.

Didn't expect. Jump back. Press body flat to wall. Fight urge to scream. To run as fast as I can

Wouldn't make it far. Not like this. Still weak. Still recovering from medications. Being tied to bed.

Strange sensation. Starts in chest.

Expect heart to pound. Fear to grip. To warn my body of danger. Imminent. Near.

But, doesn't happen. Opposite reaction. No adrenaline. Instead, heart slows. Finds steadier rhythm. Muscles release tension. Lulled into false security. Trembling limbs still. Calm. Lungs relax. Makes it easier to breathe.

Don't understand. *Shouldn't be happening. Wrong. So very wrong.* Know that.

Happens anyway.

No. Close eyes. Will her to go away. To leave me alone. To get out of my head.

Not real. Not there. Not possible.

A giggle. Amused. Oddly innocent. Somehow seductive, too. Rings in my ears. Sends goosebumps across my skin. Tingling starts in toes. In fingertips.

"Come to me, Riley," she commands. *"Don't keep me waiting."*

Never again, answer hallucination. Not that stupid. Not willing to meet her demands.

Followed her down the rabbit hole before. Big mistake. Worst I ever made. Not drinking her poison. Not ignoring warning signs. Not this time.

I can't.

"Oh, but you can."

Swallow. Steel nerves. Flex hands. Ball into fists.

"And, you will."

Have to get out of here. That's the plan. Escape this place. Get away. From Doctor. From Braxton. From Andrew.

From her.

From Wonderland.

No more restraints. No more drugs. No more liars and cruel monsters.

Certain now. What she is. What she did. What she wants. What she'll do again.

Shake head. Try to clear thoughts. Focus on truth in fragments.

She'll hurt me. Use me. Drain me. Break me into a million pieces. Kill me. Take everything she can.

"You can't resist me, Big Boy." Sudden tug in abdomen. Body lurches up. Pulled taught by string. Away from wall. Onto unsteady feet. *"I feel you trying. It's pointless. You couldn't resist me at the bar. And now, you're mine. I already told you that. You won't win."*

Find self stepping forward. Automatic. Guided by unseen hand.

Not telling body to do that. Doing it on its own. One stride. Then, another. Following siren song to her. Propelling self toward decimation.

Stop! I protest. Strain against pull. Think hard. Command arms. Legs. Manage to stumble. Not halt. Too hard to resist. *Don't do it,* I urge. *Be strong. Brave. Fight!*

Feet don't listen.

"I know you, Riley. Better than you know yourself. You poor, lost, miserable little creature. So broken, even before I sank my claws into you. Ruined by a woman who didn't deserve you. Dragged along by a shitty friend."

Wander through swinging double doors. Into waiting room. Rows of neatly arranged plastic chairs.

Patients waiting. Scrolling on phones. Watching tv. Arguing with reception.

Change of plan.

Not worried about them. Being caught. Being sent back. Need them now. To notice. To intervene. To break her hold. Take me to my room. My bed.

To Doctor. Man who wants to help. Maybe he can. Maybe…

"That's not how this works." Stronger tug. Sends me staggering toward the exit. *"Your soul is mine. Every last delicious drop that's left. Your body. Your mind. Or, did you forget?"*

Open mouth to call out. To give self away. To beg for aid.

"I've tasted you, Riley. Not just your essence. That juicy cock of yours. Those pouty little lips. And, your brain. Your mind belongs to me, Big Boy. Always. There's no going back now."

Mouth opens and closes. Like fish gasping for water. Words won't come out. Try and fail repeatedly.

Lodge in throat. Choking me. Suffocating me. Leading me to the end.

"Honestly, this is sad. I let you rest, but now I'm lonely. It's time to play again. Come outside."

Get out! Get out of head!

"Naughty boy. I'll be sure to punish you."

Chuckles again. Harsh. Menacing. Wicked.

"Riley?" Voice comes from behind me.

Doctor Barrows. Try to face him. Get halfway. Spine snaps back.

Can't. Keep walking forward. Stilted movements. Mechanical steps.

Quickly, approaches. Stays several feet away. Hands stretched out. Like when we met. Sign of peace. Asking me to stop. To listen.

Open mouth again. Want to tell him. Make him help. Lead me away.

Comes out growl. Something evil. Dangerous. Deadly.

"Riley, please," he tries. "You shouldn't be out here. It's not safe. We need to get you back to your room. I don't know how you found your way into the lobby, but this area is off-limits. Do you understand?"

Understand. Agree. Please, Doctor. Help me. Take me back!

Getting closer to entrance. To outside. To freedom I craved. No longer desire.

Let me go! Evil bitch!

"No." One little word. Same one I said to Braxton. Laced with venom.

Too close now. Set off sensors.

Automatic doors slide open. Night sky outside. Breeze wafts in. Brushes up against cheeks. Bare arms. Neck.

"Don't do this, Riley," Doctor begs. Reaches for me. Reconsiders. Afraid I'll attack.

Like I did before. To him. To Nurse. To Andrew. To Braxton.

What have I become?

Buzzing returns. In my skull. In my ears. On my skin.

Driving me mad.

"Oh, baby... You're already mad," she whispers. *"I made sure of that."*

Pull too strong. Can't resist. Breaks remaining self-control down. Drags me over threshold.

Doctor cuts me off. Moves in front. Blocks path with body. Calls for help.

"Please, Riley. I can't help you if you try to leave. I won't be able to convince them to withhold sedatives or restraints. I've been fighting for you. Believe me! And, I'll keep fighting for you. You just have to turn back."

But, she's right there.

Across the street. Under shadow of tree. Watching me with narrow red eyes.

Light up like fire. Flash when she blinks. Raises hand. Points finger. Curls at self. Asserts her will. Reels me in.

Fury overtakes me. Rage I can't control. Hands fly out. Slam into Doctor's shoulders. Send him tumbling back.

Lands on sidewalk. Sprawled on all fours. Scrambles to right self.

Not fast enough.

Step over Doctor. Onto curb. Blink at woman who ruined life.

Purses her lips. Blows a kiss. Winks one of those gorgeous eyes.

"Yes," she whispers. *"That's right. Come, Riley. You know you want to. Come to me."*

Abandon sidewalk. On the asphalt. Moving closer. Holding breath.

Bright lights. Not in front of me. To the side. Growing larger. Moving fast.

Red. White. Blinking. Flashing.

Shrill horn. Honking. Blasting.

Smile turns up her lips.

"Riley, no!" Doctor bellows. Races toward me. Reaches. Tries to grab.

Snakelike tongue flicks against her chin.

Shattering pain. Feet leave ground.

Body flying. Rolling. Crashing. Crushing. Snapping

Numb.

Black.

EPILOGUE

BRAXTON

The funeral director takes his place behind the white podium and adjusts the microphone into the correct position. It crackles to life, sending quiet static through the speakers at each corner of the room. Subtly, he clears his throat, and without having to raise his voice, captures the crowd's attention.

The assembled mourners and gawkers cease their conversations and turn to face him expectantly. The low hum that filled the room seconds before becomes too quiet for comfort.

For a moment, the director says nothing but rather stares down at several notecards he's arranged before himself. He studies their contents, shifting them as he does. The papers make muted scraping sounds as he slides them across the polished wood.

No one interrupts this process. All are still. Intrigued or respectful. Fascinated or reverent.

"On behalf of Lutwidge and Dodgson, we would like to thank you for joining us here this evening to remember Riley Sylers," he finally begins. Before continuing, he adjusts his striped tie and the small white rosebud tucked into his pocket. When he's finished, he lays his hands on the raised bezel for support. "We are honored to be here at your side as you celebrate the life and mourn the passing of this extraordinary young man who touched so many." The director looks up from his notes, face schooled into a practiced expression of sympathy. "The loss of one so young is always difficult to process, especially for those like you who loved him most."

The director lets his gaze rove over the assembly, briefly pausing on each in turn. Not wanting to see it land on me, I look away, turning my eyes to the small golden urn on the pedestal up front.

My cheeks burn, but I make no effort to hide the color saturating them. I'm not embarrassed. Far from it, in fact. What I am is confused, and angry, and sad, and so fucking disgusted with myself.

I don't want this man's pity. I don't want anyone's pity. I don't deserve it. Not a single goddamn ounce. If it weren't for me, Riley would still be alive. He'd be sucking down stale beer and gorging himself on subpar pizza. He'd be miserable, sure. Heartbroken, probably. But, he'd be here. Still moping, but still breathing.

So, fuck pity. I should be the subject of the man's scorn, not his concern.

"We must remember in this time of pain that Riley was more than just his final moments. It's far too easy to forget that in his twenty-nine years, he lived a full life on this Earth. He has touched many in profound ways, made a positive impact on his community, and leaves behind a legacy of goodness. This is what we strive to recognize in his absence. This is the reason your hearts are broken."

The director's voice warps as it fills my ears, expanding and contracting, echoing through the large room. He drones on about Riley's childhood and his adolescent years, giving a shoddy summary of his shining moments. Basketball championships. Summer camps. Train rides and Halloween costumes. Some in the audience chuckle when he takes several moments to recount a few humorous stories.

I barely listen, letting my mind wander and studying the metal vessel before me. I picked it out for him. Riley's mom couldn't manage to do it. She kept breaking down in tears every time the man showed her another option.

Her barely concealed sobs punctuate the director's every word.

It's so small. You'd think I would remember the size, right? But, now that this is happening, I barely recall holding it in my hands, turning it over and over in the display room.

It's too small, really. How could they have fit all that remains of Riley inside of it? I mean, he wasn't a large man, but he wasn't that tiny, either. To think that his body has been rendered into nothing but ash, to so little… My mind can't rectify this fact with the man I knew.

Then again, there wasn't much left of him in the end. Not after the ambulance. Riley was utterly and completely broken. That's why his mother chose cremation in the first place.

Numbness creeps into my limbs as I let this new reality sink into my thoughts.

"…and in the four years he spent at his university, Riley was a devoted member of many community service organizations. Notably, he helped start an on-campus food pantry for college students who had limited access to healthy meals. This organization continues to thrive nearly a decade later, in no small part thanks to his efforts and those of his fellow classmate and friend, Braxton Lory."

The mention of my name drags me back from my confused reverie. I swallow, forcing myself to sit tall while the crowd begins to quietly murmur.

Riley's death has become a scandal. Something whispered about when the rabble thinks no one else is listening. Every last one of them knows what happened at the hospital. It's been all over the news. "Good Samaritan Turned Attempted Murderer, Dies By Suicide" had been the headline the following morning. "Doctor Holds Dying Patient As He Passes" had been the one immediately after. Then, "Seriously Falling Standard Of Medical Care At St. Ambrose."

His name, once a symbol of courage and strength, now represents the image of a young man irrevocably fallen.

The fresh gauze covering the healing wound on my neck peeks out from beneath my shirt, providing damning evidence to support the fucking narrative. I tried to hide it, but the injury is too sizable to conceal without the bandage, and the gauze is too bulky to tuck under my collar.

The director ignores the whispers, forging on with his carefully prepared story. I'm sure this isn't the first unsavory visitation he's had to oversee in his career. It won't be the last one, either.

"Riley's giving nature did not falter after his graduation. Rather, it flourished, as can be seen through his career. Using his degree in architecture to work alongside the city to restore many beloved buildings that had fallen into disrepair, Riley Sylers became a hero to many. Families found new homes. Local senior citizens gained a new community center. Perhaps most importantly, Allan Elementary's campus reopened, not as it was, but as a technologically advanced facility that provides education and safety to non-traditional students who have faced struggles far greater than many of our own."

From several rows behind me, Doctor Barrows clears his throat. His presence tonight came as a surprise. I'm still shocked he bothered to come. After losing his job at the hospital because of the media coverage, I thought he'd hate Riley and me. Guess not, though. He's a better person than anyone gives him credit for.

A better man than me. He should have been rewarded for the way he treated Riley, not punished. But, this world is fucked.

I'm tempted to turn around and face him, to offer my support, but that would be inappropriate. Even without looking, I know there are still many people staring at my back. Waiting for me to do something stupid. That's why I chose to sit in the front row, so I wouldn't have to see them.

Doctor Barrows hadn't gotten so lucky. By the time he'd arrived, the chairs near me were already full. He has to bear their scrutiny. I don't want to make it worse for him.

Still, I can't help but angle my body slightly in his direction. From the corner of my eye, I catch the anxiety-driven rhythm of his bouncing knee. Andrew sits beside him, ever the bodyguard, apparently a friend as well as a former co-worker, remaining stoic.

"In the days, weeks, and months to come, hold on to this courageous young man who found room in his heart for so many. Do not let the modern world tarnish his light. Remember Riley as he lived, not as he died. Honor his efforts, and take solace in the lives that will forever be better because he cared enough to intervene. Above all, keep his journey going. That's what Riley would have wanted. That's what he lived for."

"Amen," someone I don't recognize chimes in from farther down the row. My best guess? She's one of the people he worked with. Probably runs the old folks' home or whatever. Others echo the sentiment, but I keep my mouth shut, dropping my gaze to the floor.

"Please, take all the time you need this evening to seek comfort in each other and make peace with the difficult road ahead. Our parlor will remain open to guests until nine pm. In the main hall, we've provided light refreshments and fresh water. Remember to care for your bodies as well as your souls. Tomorrow morning at eleven am, Riley will be carried to his final resting place in Memorial Gardens. You're welcome to join us here as we escort him on this closing journey."

Finished with his speech, the director scoops up the stack of cards. These, he quickly tucks into the breast pocket of his vest, removing them from sight.

"My name is Charles, and I'll be passing through to ensure you all have everything you need. Don't hesitate to stop me if you have any questions or concerns."

With that, Charles steps back from the podium, then unlocks the wheels at the base with his foot. He pauses, leaving a fitting amount of time for the guests to disengage from his presence. The assembly does exactly that. Silently, he tows his podium toward the side of the room and tucks it away behind a thick maroon curtain while none watch.

Unlike the rest of the crowd, I remain seated. They ignore me, scuttling off to find another to talk to or to visit the minuscule urn. I should do the same, but my body's too heavy, too weighed down with the burden of a guilty conscience, to force myself to stand. I can't convince myself to do anything more than count the threads of the worn carpet beneath my soles.

Time passes in a blur.

"Riley's death is not your fault," Doctor Barrows offers as I reach thread three hundred and seventy-one.

I hadn't heard him approach, but his proximity isn't entirely unexpected. We're the talk of the town, two of the three pariahs, the last ones standing. It makes sense that he'd seek me out.

I don't bother to reply. I just shake my head and keep up my counting. Focus on a task I can handle. On something concrete, physical, simple. Controlled.

Doctor Barrows doesn't mind my silence. He's a patient person. I gathered that much before everything went to shit at the hospital. But, he doesn't give up, either. No, he stays with me and settles into the chair to my left. The cushion lets out a reticent "shush" as it deflates beneath his form.

"Mr. Lory, I think we both know that, despite what speculation and my superiors claim, there was nothing either of us could have done to prevent what happened when Riley stepped through those doors and into the street. You were gravely injured, receiving life-sustaining medical care, and I had no way of reaching him before he found his way onto the asphalt."

"Does it fucking matter?" I ask. "Riley didn't deserve to die like that," I say. Tears flood my eyes, and I lose count of my distraction. "No one does." I blink back the moisture threatening to spill down my face.

I'm not going to cry. Not here. Not in front of them. I won't show them weakness.

"That is also true," Doctor Barrows concurs. "But, you must know that it was what happened to your friend the night he went missing that drove him into traffic, Mr. Lory. It was not your insistence that he visit the bar, nor was it inadequate care on my part. Your friend's mind was delicate… shattered. That's what took his life. Trauma, not your actions or your choices."

Anger thrums in my chest, not at the doctor, but at the partial truth I refuse to accept behind his words.

"He wouldn't have gone missing if I'd let him stay home. I took him to The Rabbit Hole. I left him there so I could get laid. And when he needed me, I wasn't there. So, I may not have pushed Riley in front of an ambulance, but I certainly got him killed. You won't convince me otherwise."

"Perhaps." Doctor Barrows sighs and fiddles with the sleeve of his shirt. "But, we have no way of knowing that for certain. Who's to say fate didn't have its sights set on Mr. Sylers that evening? Hmm? Who's to say we as humans have any control over the way our ending comes at all?"

I can't help but laugh at his notion. "I thought you were a man of science," I spit. "Fate is just a thing people like us blame for all our fuck ups, Doctor. It's a scapegoat."

At this, he falls silent. The doctor's head tips back as he studies the tiled ceiling above us. For several moments, he stays that way, contemplating thoughts I can't fathom. I can see the wheels turn in his mind until finally, he closes his eyes and smiles.

"I consider myself a dabbler in both." The doctor chuckles, a sound completely at odds with his sad expression. "It is my belief that one cannot exist without the other, Mr. Lory. What is it that Shakespeare said? 'There are more things in heaven and earth than are dreamt of in your philosophy.' And, there are. I've seen enough to know that for certain."

"Well, you'll have to excuse me if I don't give a shit what Shakespeare thinks today. I'm more concerned with my dead friend than an ancient poet's words."

"I do forgive you, Mr. Lory. But, it's not me who needs to offer forgiveness. Not to you or to anyone else." Doctor Barrows locks eyes with me. He places his palm over my knee and squeezes reassuringly. "I want you to consider something. Spare me a moment of incredulity if you will. I'm asking you to think about life as a whole."

Now, it's my turn to laugh. "Oh, here we go."

"I do not believe life is pointless. Nor do I think it's easy," Doctor Barrows forges on. "Or for the faint-hearted. It can be cruel and devastating, but it can also be wonderful and astonishing. The truth lies in the moments."

Riley's mom shuffles past us, sparing us only the briefest of looks.

"Some moments in life make you larger, Mr. Lory," he offers. "They build you up, mold you into a proud and strong person. Those are the moments everyone searches for. Milestones and achievements. The way you compare yourself to others. Falling in love. Getting the promotion. Winning the lottery. What have you. But, it can't always be that way. If it was, we wouldn't appreciate the good things. So, some moments make you smaller too, leave you feeling insignificant and lost. Tear you down until you're nothing but sinew and bones. But, here's the thing: we have to keep going. We must keep wandering down new paths toward the unknown. And, the unknown is beautiful. Terrifying, sure. But, necessary. Because none of us know where we're going before we meet death, and if you don't know where you're going, any road can take you somewhere extraordinary."

Doctor Barrows pushes away from his chair and stands in front of me before continuing. He extends his hand, offering to help me out of my seat. Too proud to take it, I shove myself up to stand beside him on my own.

"Death is inevitable." The doctor gestures at Riley's urn. "We're all going to die. Some of us sooner than others. Too soon, you might say. God knows I've had my fair share of patients leave this world, young and old alike. Friends and family, too. So, we fear death, but we can't fight it. Life isn't like that. Life is a choice."

"Riley didn't choose to die. I don't care what the news says. He didn't commit suicide. He would never."

"I don't believe he did either, but you're missing the concept. See, we choose life every time we draw in a breath. Every time we eat. Buy the new car. Take the vacation. Have sex. Take a shot at something — anything."

Frustration overtakes me. I try to stop myself, but before I can, nasty words escape my mouth. "Can you get to the fucking point?"

Doctor Barrows is unfazed by my reaction. He just nods and says, "You chose life that night, Mr. Lory. Was it the right choice? I don't know. No one does. But, you can't fault yourself for living. You can't carry the weight of your friend's loss. You have to keep choosing life. Keep exploring the new roads."

Behind us, the doors to the visitation room open and softly close.

"I'm going to find out what happened to Riley, Doctor Barrows. I'm not just going to fuck off and live life like none of this ever happened. If that's what you're suggesting..."

"Certainly not," he responds. "I don't have any more answers about what happened to your friend than you do. Believe me, I haven't stopped searching, either. Without the hospital, my resources are limited. That's no help, and we both know the police would rather sweep this under the rug. But, what I can do is choose to put my faith in time. I can keep living while searching. I can find a new job. Move to a new city. Go on an adventure now that I don't have the limitations of employment. Do you understand?"

"Sure," I tell him. "But, I can't do that. Not until I have answers."

"Time has all the answers. Time doesn't run out like we think it does. Time is eternal. It will be here long after you and I. Someday, I hope it gives us the truth. But until then, we must keep going."

Andrew approaches the doctor and whispers something into the man's ear. I can't make out what he says, but Doctor Barrows shakes his head and frowns disapprovingly.

"The media has arrived outside, Mr. Lory. Unfortunately, that means it's time for me to go. I don't want my presence here to undermine the healing that needs to occur. Please, let me know if you need anything."

My eyes flash to the back of the rows of chairs where the exit waits. Without looking at him, I nod. "I will."

"Anything at all. I mean that. Truly. And, I'm sorry for your loss and your sorrows. Know that as well."

"I do."

"Good." Doctor Barrows claps me on the back, then allows Andrew to steer him to the side door.

No one notices when he leaves. No one but me. The only remaining pariah rooted to this spot on the floor.

I'm still staring at the sealed doors when a gentle tap on my shoulder catches me off guard.

"I'm sorry about your friend," a familiar voice says. "He seemed like a really good guy."

Turning to face her, I see the fucking bartender, all dressed up in black mourning clothes. Her blonde hair has been braided and wrapped around the base of her skull into a tight bun. Absent the apron and tight t-shirt, she looks almost normal. Almost.

"What are you doing here?" I demand, suddenly filled with rage at the sight of her. "You don't belong here unless you're ready to tell me what happened to Riley at your shithole bar."

The bartender sighs and looks at her shoes. "I don't know anything the news hasn't already reported," she answers. Her hand slips down to her hip, and her thumb slides into the pocket of her slacks. "He left before my shift ended. I was there until two, pouring drinks."

"Yeah, right," I accuse.

After Riley died, I went back to The Rabbit Hole again. I tore that whole damn building apart. I questioned the employees, dumped out trash cans, dove into the dumpster, stalked behind the bar, and even went so far as to barge into the backrooms.

I didn't find anything. Not one single clue that might tell me what happened to him when I left.

But, she wasn't there. It was her day off, the manager claimed. That doesn't sit right with me. It's too convenient. Too clean.

"I know you saw something," I growl. "You had to."

"I wish I had," she responds. Her golden eyes stare up at me through thick lashes, and she blinks solemnly. "Look, I just thought it would be nice to offer my condolences since I was there the night things fell apart. If you want me gone, I'll go."

I open my mouth to scream at the woman, but before I do, a new thought seizes me. Grabs me by the throat and takes hold.

This is an opportunity.

"No, I'm sorry," I say, attempting to smooth over my rude words. "Stay if you want. I'm not doing so great right now. I'm sure you understand."

"Of course," she says. A tight-lipped smile spreads across her mouth. "These things are horrible, and then everyone thinks they know how you feel and they can fix it. It's bullshit."

"Yeah," I grumble. Watching her. Waiting for a glimpse of the truth.

The bartender shifts to look over her shoulder toward the back of the room and the doors. "Did you want to get out of here? Maybe we could go somewhere for coffee? I'm not on the clock until ten tonight. We could talk about your friend?" Her voice trails off, considering. Then, she turns back to face me. "I usually meet up with Chester at the cafe down the block before my shift. He's my ride. You're welcome to join us."

"Chester?"

The bartender laughs. Fucking laughs, like she's as carefree as can be. "The bouncer. You know, the one who sits at the door."

"Oh, Antonio," I offer. "He hates my guts."

She doesn't even flinch when I call him by the wrong name. "He hates everyone, but I'll make him play nice, just this once." The bartender reaches for my hand, and I let her twine her fingers with mine. Much like the funeral director's had, her face morphs into a mask of sympathy and pity. "Come on. Funerals are for the dead. Let's go someplace nicer, huh? You can tell me all about him."

A strange tingling begins where her skin brushes against me.

Anticipation, probably. Excitement. Hope. Because one way or another, I'm going to get to the bottom of this. I'm going to find out what happened to Riley. If it kills me, I'll make her tell me what she knows.

She leads me through the rows toward the exit.

Snow swirls in the air as I leave the funeral home behind me. Multitudes of news vans crowd the too-narrow curb. I spare one look back to Lutwidge and Dodgson, and I could swear I see Riley on the steps leading away from the road.

His face is stricken, filled with sorrow. A mask of fear and dread. His lips mouth words I can't hear. His arm lifts, reaching in my direction, begging for me to save him.

Don't worry, man, I tell him, hoping his spirit can read my thoughts. *Whoever did this is going to pay for it. I promise.*

And just like that, his specter is gone.

All that remains is me and the bartender as we wind our way toward answers.

THANK YOU FOR READING!

Thank you for reading *Wicked Little Rabbit,* the first installment in For the Dark and Depraved. I hope you have enjoyed this work.

Do you have questions for the author? If so, reach out to me at smoran@obsidianinkwell.com and you might have them answered!

Please feel free to leave an honest review on Amazon or Goodreads. I look forward to writing for you again soon!

Want more from Samantha Moran? Don't forget to sign up for her newsletter at samanthamoran.net!

Keep reading for an excerpt from Samantha Moran's award-winning novella, *Dealings in the Dark,* and be sure to check out her list of published works!

QUESTIONS FOR THE AUTHOR

Q) What inspired you to write a horror retelling of *Alice in Wonderland*?

A) Well, for one thing, I've always loved *Alice in Wonderland*, from the original book to the media adaptations. Getting the chance to explore the mind-boggling adventures from a new perspective was like a dream! It's amazing how things are never what they seem to be in Alice's universe, and that gives me as an author free rein over an entire world of curious things!

But, the real inspiration for this book in particular came from my first ever major book event, Sinful Signings in Roanoke, VA. I had a blast there in 2023 and met some incredibly talented romance writers. The theme for the second year of the convention is the origins of Dark Romance, and I thought to myself, what could be darker than a horror and thriller retelling with spice? Plus, the reader to whom this book is dedicated wanted a sexy and twisted tale, so I had to give it to her!

Anyway, I decided to give it a try, even though I wasn't very comfortable with writing naughty things because of my past career as an educator. It ended up being quite fun! I think I blushed more writing this book than I ever have before, and that's saying something!

Q) Why did you choose to make "Alice" the villain instead of the protagonist?

A) There are two sides to this question. The simple answer is, why not? I absolutely love writing a good villain. In fact, in most of my books, my villain ends up being my favorite character to write because they can be so unapologetically vicious.

So, on the one hand, I wanted to twist the narrative. I wanted to create a villainess who took no shit and got exactly what she needed, regardless of everyone else. My succubus, Allison, is exactly that. She warns the boys away, and they don't listen, so she does what she wants with my main character and lets him deal with the consequences. Since succubi are sexually charged demons, casting Allison in this role made perfect sense.

The more complex and essential answer is that I also wanted this book to contain important social commentary, especially involving sexual assault as it occurs among men. Too often, there is a misconception that men cannot be raped and that women cannot be rapists. This is 100% not the case.

While the vast majority of sexual assault victims are female (estimated ninety to ninety-one percent), rape is not a biological sex-specific issue. In fact, according to Rainn.org, one in ten sexual assault victims are male. Additionally, roughly three percent of the male population in the United States have experienced attempted sexual assault or a completed rape. This data only comes from reported cases. Many never speak out about their experience at all.

Furthermore, I wanted to shine a light on how damaging sexual assault can be to the human psyche. It can cause a devastating loss of self that should never be overlooked.

So, I hope this book can bring awareness to these important issues and help us move into a safer future for everyone.

Q) What is a Kaibyo?

Chester, Allison's personal guard and the bouncer from The Rabbit Hole, is a personalization of the Cheshire Cat. Because of this, I wanted him to have demonic significance. So, when I went digging and learned about the creature known as Kaibyo, I knew it was the perfect fit!

Kaibyo are Japanese cat demons, a type of Yokai. One subset of Kaibyo are Kasha, specifically known as body snatchers. So, Chester became Allison's confidant and employee, the one who hides her secrets and keeps her safe by discarding her corpses and wrangling in her discarded "broken men."

Q) What was the experience like writing with so many intentional fragments?

A) As a former English teacher, this was particularly challenging! I kept wanting to go back and address the fragments. However, the way the main character thinks and speaks is an important component of his personality. The things he went through severely damaged his psyche, and he simply could not think and speak as fluidly as everyone else. If I hadn't portrayed him in this manner, his suffering would not have been as clear. Still, it was like pulling teeth!

Q) Why did you wait so long to tell us the main character's name? And, why did Doctor Barrows decided to use the name "James?"

A) My main character needed to be lost. As literally as he could, he fell down the rabbit hole and ended up in a nightmare inducing world of terror, the victim of a depraved succubus. She took everything from him, physically and mentally, and that included his self-awareness. Not giving him a name reduced him to something pitiful. That's exactly what he needed to be.

Doctor Barrows wanted so badly to see the main character recover from his trauma. When I wrote him, I intended for him to be an incredibly compassionate, if ineffective, caregiver. There was nothing he could have done to save my main character, even if he had been given the time. But, since he was a good soul, he didn't want to refer to my main character as "John Doe" like someone who was deceased, nor did he think it appropriate to consistently refer to him as "the patient," which would have been dehumanizing. Doctor Barrows is a balance to everything that was taken from Riley.

As for the name "James," in early 2024, it ranks number ten among most popular names. Therefore, it would be considered common, and while somewhat impersonal, still preferable to nothing for Doctor Barrows and Riley.

Q) This was your first attempt at writing explicit sexual content. What was that like? Was it difficult to approach it from a male perspective?

A) At first, writing explicit content was difficult. I barely managed to convince myself to put my fingers to the keys to type out the naughty scenes. However, I had very encouraging friends and family members, so I decided to give it a try. It ended up being fun in the end.

Approaching the story from the male perspective was a bit tricky because I had to step outside of my own experience. So, I enlisted the help of several male alpha readers to make sure the content I included was as authentic to their experiences as it could be. I will forever appreciate them!

The hardest parts of this book to write were the assault scenes because I am a survivor myself. I needed to demonstrate the horrific qualities of Allison as a demon, but I hated to put my character through it.

Q) What happens to Braxton? Will you ever tell us?

Nope! That's my secret, and I'm keeping it. *Wink* Who knows? You might see him again, or he might be Allison's next victim. That's the beauty of a cliffhanger, isn't it?

Q) Will there be more stories like this in the future? If so, which fairytales do you plan to reimagine?

A) If everything goes according to plan, yes! I have thoughts regarding several more twisted, spicy horror and thriller retellings of our childhood favorite tales in the For the Dark and Depraved collection! In particular, I have some general ideas for *The Little Mermaid, Sleeping Beauty,* and *Rumpelstiltskin*! Stick around for more tales, and sign up for my newsletter at samanthamoran.net/newsletter for monthly updates!

RESOURCES FOR SURVIVORS OF SEXUAL ASSAULT

As I mentioned in the "Questions for the Author" section of this book, bringing awareness to the prevalence and effects of sexual assault and dispelling the misconception that assault cannot happen to men is incredibly important to me.

If you have been a victim of sexual assault, whether attempted or completed, know that you are not alone. I see you, and I believe you. It is not your fault, and how you choose to proceed is no one's business but your own.

However, there are help centers available to you. Here, I have compiled a list of a few resources for those who are faced with matters of sexual assault to use as a starting point for their journey.

Please know that I am not a licensed therapist or medical professional. These are intended solely for guidance, and I recommend that you do your own research. Furthermore, I hope you find someone who you can trust and confide in, be that a family member, friend, health professional, or law enforcement officer.

I wish you peace and recovery.

National Sexual Support Hotline:
Rainn.org
800-656-4673

National Domestic Violence Hotline:
thehotline.org
800-799-7233

Joyful Heart Foundation:
joyfulheartfoundation.org
212-475-2026

Victim Connect Resource Center
victimconnect.org
855-484-2846

ACKNOWLEDGMENTS

I would like to offer a special thank you to those individuals who have made this novel possible.

Thank you to my friends Kassie G., Desie R., and Autumn S. who inspired me to delve into the world of erotic horror. I've always been drawn to the darkness, but I never thought I'd write a book with so much naughty content. It was a lot of fun, and I'm looking forward to writing more!

> For Kassie G. specifically, thank you for letting me dedicate this one to you.

> For Desie R. specifically, thanks for reading my chapters as they were drafted. Your excitement and enthusiasm was EVERYTHING!

> For Autumn S. specifically, thank you for hyping me up about my first spicy release! I might have turned back on it without you!

Thank you to Caytlyn Brooke, my friend and fellow author, for inspiring me with her books and sharing in my passion along this journey. Your gingerbread man was my first enjoyable foray into twisted, spicy tales. He was delicious. Allison is something else entirely, but I hope she leaves you hungry for more, just like your wicked dessert did to me.

Thank you to Brian Scala, my friend and fellow author, for alpha reading and always encouraging me to keep writing. 2023 was a rough year, and because of your friendship, I overcame the obstacles set before me. You were always a message away, never in doubt of my abilities, and one of the most supportive people I know. #DawnRiders

Thank you to Evie Black, my friend and fellow author, for beta reading for this release. Your comments were great, and your feedback was incredibly helpful! I'm so glad you wanted to be a part of this team.

Thank you to my friend Marissa C. for alpha reading, too! You're always an amazing hype woman. I probably wouldn't have any books without you!

And of course, thank you to my husband John for alpha reading, walking me through those cheek-reddening moments, holding my hand through the difficult scenes, and refusing to let me give up. I can write profanity all day long, and horror and thriller are my jam, but when it comes to naughty words, I am far less than a pro. Your gentle encouragement means the world. I love you more than you'll ever know. You will forever have my heart and soul.

Thank you to my reader group, Coven of Chaos, on Facebook! You guys are incredible!

Thank you to every single person who pre-ordered this release. You made this book possible.

Thank you to my son for taking naps when I needed him to! Toddlers aren't known for their cooperation, but you were a real MVP, buddy.

Thank you to my daughter for telling me to never give up writing until I'm 111 years old! As long as I have you in my corner, there's nothing I can't do, baby.

Thank you to my ARC readers! We cut it close to the deadline with this one, but you pulled through all the same. You rock!

Lastly, thank you to my readers for picking up this book and seeing it through to the end. I appreciate each of you more than you know. You've changed my life, and I will never forget it. Without you, pursuing my dream wouldn't be possible.

BONUS CONTENT

As a thank you for your time, please enjoy this bonus content. Happy hauntings and happy reading!

"THERE ARE RULES, ALEXANDRIA.
I WILL NOT ALLOW THEM TO BE BROKEN."

Dealings in the Dark

BOOK ONE OF
THE CURSED SOULS SERIES

SAMANTHA MORAN

DEALINGS IN THE DARK:
CHAPTER ONE

The box in my hand rattles as I quickly walk down my old road beneath the light of an early autumn moon. The stars in the sky tonight are absolutely stunning. The air is still warm and humid, and the leaves have just begun to change. There is a refreshing breeze that causes the branches of the old willows to sway back and forth, almost as if they are dancing. The bits of gravel under my feet crunch against the soles of my worn Chucks, announcing my presence to anyone and anything that cares enough to listen.

Were I out here for any other reason, I might find my stroll enjoyable, leisurely even. I might listen to the frogs and crickets in the swampy underbrush tell their stories of the day. I might sit underneath one of the willows and drink a hot cider. I've done those things many times before.

But tonight, nothing about this walk is enjoyable. Every movement in the shadows makes me jump. Every crunch in the woods steals my breath and makes my whole body buzz with anxiety. I need to get this done, fast. The night is not safe anymore.

I hear a strangled whisper in the distance as the creature calls out my name. I'm not stupid enough to turn around and look, not this time. It almost had me before. I won't acknowledge it again. If I do, it will mean the end for me. The creature has caught my scent and has been stalking me for weeks. If it knows I can hear it, that I can see it, it will only make the hunt that much more thrilling. There will be no help for me.

I'm not ready to die.

The sounds of running water fill my ears as I approach the creek and the road veers sharply off to the left. I follow the path, staying as close to the water and as far away from the trees on the other side as the road allows.

For whatever reason, the creature is afraid of the water. Whenever I approach the creek, it always backs away. The sounds of its strangled cries grow softer as the creek burbles. I allow myself one deep breath to calm my nerves as I hug the water's edge. I relish the sense of momentary safety. It won't last long.

Before me, the road splits into a fork. To the left, it hugs the bank of the creek and promises continued safety, but that is not the path that I need to follow.

I hold the cigar box tightly to my chest as I test the wood of an old rickety bridge that leads off the right. I haven't crossed this bridge in years, not since I was young. The boards squeak in protest as I step forward, but to my relief, they bear my weight.

I move slowly, tip-toeing from one board to the next and stepping over the places where planks have fallen into the water below. The bridge isn't long or terribly high, and the creek isn't deep, but it is fast-moving right now, and if I were to fall in here, I would be in serious trouble. There's no one who would find me here, at least until the morning.

I'm running out of time. I don't know how long the water will keep the beast at bay. Not indefinitely, I'm sure. I can't do this with the creature on my heels.

As I reach the end of the bridge and step onto the clay path on the other side, I desperately want to turn around to see if the beast has abandoned its hunt. My whole body fights to do so as I continue to force it forward toward my destination against every instinct of self-preservation. Out here, alone in the dark, I am easy prey, and leaving my back unguarded feels so very wrong.

I pick up speed, ducking underneath wild overgrowth and dodging debris from the last thunderstorm. The scents of decayed leaves and wet soil overwhelm my senses. I'm almost there. Almost.

Ahead, I can see my destination. Like a guardian, the old one-room schoolhouse looms over a four-way split in the path, the structure long since abandoned. In the light of the moon, it casts a shadow so long that the path is almost consumed. The school's double doors swing on their rusty hinges, grinding and groaning with the light breeze.

No one has cared for or claimed this space in years. It's perfect for what I must do now. There will be no interruptions or distractions.

Eager to reach my destination, I break into a run, and the rattling of the box intensifies as its contents bounce against the thin cedar sides. Thirty feet, twenty feet, ten. I skid to a halt at the center of the crossroads and fall to my knees, out of breath. Stones planted deep within the clay dig into my shins painfully, but I don't care. I made it to the crossing. The first part of my task is complete. I tentatively let out a sigh of relief.

I shift on my knees, twisting to retrieve an old spade and a lighter from my back pocket. I drop the lighter on the ground beside me. I use my hands to clear away the rocks and sticks in front of me before retrieving the spade and piercing it into the clay repeatedly, loosening the soil until I can dig up the earth and pile it by the side of the hole.

Once the hole is deep enough, I drop the spade beside the lighter and open the cigar box. I scan the contents again, just to make sure that nothing was lost on my journey. It's all there: dandelion leaves, wormwood, mandrake root, smoky quartz, a lock of my hair, a large black candle, and a small vial of my blood. I pull the candle out of the box and close it up, then place the box into the hole, burying it and patting the clay down firmly on top.

My hands shake as I place the candle atop the freshly turned earth. I close my eyes and feel for the lighter, lifting it up and squeezing it firmly in my hand. I pray to whoever might be listening that this will work. It has to. I don't know what else to do.

"I summon thee," I whisper my command. "Cross over into this plane. Hear me." I follow this with the difficult Latin words from my grandmother's near ancient grimoire, repeating them five times, then once more uttering my command. "I summon thee. Cross over into this plane."

I flick open the lid of the Zippo, springing to life a bright blue flame. Hesitantly, I tip the flame against the wick of the candle until it catches. Smoke curls up from the flame, gray and thick. It sparks, and the flame shoots high up into the air. Black wax drips down the side and puddles onto the clay below, spreading out from the candle and spilling toward me like a winding snake. I pull myself up from my knees to stand and watch as the wax drips farther and farther away from the source until it connects with my shoe. The ritual is working.

I take a step back, then skirt the candle and approach the old building. Cautiously, I scan the inside before entering. Old wood and metal tablet desks are tipped onto their sides. The place smells of mildew and rot. A large slate board, still bearing the marks of my childhood drawings, lines the farthest wall. Moonlight streams in through holes in the ceiling and the breeze whistles through spaces between the boards.

It's empty.

I close the doors firmly behind me as I step inside, shoving an old, busted table in front of them to keep them from opening of their own accord. It isn't much, but I hope that it will at least slow the creature down when it finds me. I just need it to buy me time.

It's quiet in the one-room schoolhouse. Only the sounds of my breathing and the creaking beneath my shoes echo in the large, abandoned space. I squeeze my black tourmaline and obsidian necklace for protection, a gift from my grandmother, as I pick my way through the remains of the once-loved classroom until I reach the slate board, as far away from the doors as I can be, and I wait. I close my eyes, breathing as quietly as I can, and listen.

Moments later, a deep chuckle behind me tells me I am not alone.

Find Dealings in the Dark on Amazon

Find Dealings in the Dark at samanthamoran.net

ABOUT THE AUTHOR

Samantha Moran (she/her) is a multi-genre author primarily focused on supernatural horror, thriller, and fantasy. She is fascinated by all manner of things that go bump in the night and strives to create relatable characters who face realistic problems in fictional settings. As her motto claims, she is a firm believer in the idea that "happily ever after is overrated" and prefers her stories to be full of twists and mysteries.

Samantha holds a Bachelor's in English Secondary Education and is a proud Magna Cum Laude graduate of Western Michigan University. (Go Broncos!) She is also a loving mother of two amazing children and has been happily married to her husband since 2015. She and her family reside in southwest Michigan, though she has also previously resided in the Baltimore, Maryland area.

Samantha lives with Multiple Sclerosis which sometimes severely impacts her daily life, especially her ability to use her hands.

In her free time, she loves tarot, playing *Dungeons and Dragons*, reading books, writing, and spending time with her family and pets.

For more information about Samantha Moran, visit her website at www.samanthamoran.net.

Visit Samantha Moran's website

BOOKS BY SAMANTHA MORAN

Cursed Souls:

Dealings in the Dark, (2022)

Bound and Betrayed, (2022)

Legacy of Lies, (Coming Soon)

Standalone Works:

Tales of Grief and Healing, (2023)

The Ruin, (2023)

For the Dark and Depraved:

Wicked Little Rabbit, (2024)

The Apothecary of Curiosities Short Stories:

"Death's Nell," (2023)

"Kiss of Death," (2023)

"Deadly Delicacies," (2024)

Milton Keynes UK
Ingram Content Group UK Ltd.
UKHW010826230424
441593UK00002B/62